UNDERGROUND
ADVICE COLUMNIST

GARFIELD S. GARDNER

Copyright © 2014 by Garfield S. Gardner

All rights reserved. No part of this book may be reproduced or utilized in any form or by any means, electronic or mechanical, including photocopying, recording, or by an information storage and retrieval system, without permission in writing from the author or publisher.

Published by Dream Free or Die!℠ Press

Dream Free or Die!℠ Press was established in 2013 as an alternative to the large, commercial publishing houses and commercial self-publishing agencies currently dominating the book publishing industry. In providing a service to gifted writers toward fulfilling the dream of being published, Dream Free or Die!℠ Press operates in the interest of bringing dreams to fruition rather than private profit, and is committed to aiding our authors in publishing works of significant artistic value.

Printed in the United States of America

Library of Congress Control Number: 2014947591

ISBN 978-0-692-22935-4

Author: Garfield S. Gardner ǀ hottywoodhelps.com

Editor: Stephani E. D. McDow ǀ dreamfreeordie.com

Visual Artist: Nicole Summers ǀ artbynicole.net

Cover Graphic Design: Kevin Bright ǀ urontherise.com

Printer: Gorham Printing ǀ gorhamprinting.com

As the crisp mid-afternoon air met the vibrant sun's rays, no amount of heat – body or sunlight – was enough to melt the handcuffs from Gardner's burnt, caramel wrists. Sitting in the back of a police car for allegations of beating a degenerate, high school aged kid for attempting to steal his $2.25 change from the purchase of a Snickers bar at a local 7/11, the reflection of the squad car's flashing red and blue lights crashing against the storefront's window was enough to cause beads of sweat to roll down his perfectly groomed face. Gardner, a small town city boy and otherwise well-mannered and mildly tempered newspaper editor, found himself entangled in a fourth run-in with the law in the last five months.

"Dispatch, this is unit T56. I have a 10-15 in progress and need you to run a 10-29 on suspect George Adam Robert David Nora Edward Robert, first initial George. Suspect in custody is a black male. Age 36. Possible 10-100. Over." A freakishly young looking officer decked out in full man-in-blue gear, accessorized with handcuffs and a billy club, spewed unrecognizable cop lingo into the speaker of a two-way radio. He waited patiently for a response from the faceless voice on the other side of the CB while picking dirt out of his fingernails. Gardner, having heard these lyrics numerous times before,

Chapter 1
Set Up

Acknowledgments

I'd like to give special thanks to a few people that supported my efforts of delving into the world of authorship.

First and foremost, I want to give thanks to my Lord and Savior Jesus Christ, for without Whom none of this is possible.

Thank you, Mom, for always encouraging me to follow my dreams, and for not throwing those spiked red heels at me whenever I refused to turn off my reading lamp at night.

Thank you, Granny, for being the matriarch of our family, the light of my life, and also for being my personal bodyguard whenever Mom was ready to kick my butt when she couldn't find the spiked heels I thanked her for not throwing.

Thank you, to the Duke Ellington School of Arts, for teaching me how to harness the power of the pen. I have learned that it is definitely mightier than the sword.

Thank you, Binky, for understanding the language of Bunkese.

I cannot adequately thank all those persons who insisted I would never accomplish anything more than being popular. It is your lack of faith in me that encourages me to forever sing the song ineptly named "Nananabooboo!"

Thank you, to the police officer that let me off with a warning. I may not remember your name, but the image of your shiny badge is forever etched into my brain.

Last, but not least, I must thank my cat for taking on the responsibility of listening to me gripe when everyone else told me to shut up. It's a good thing you can't speak.

narrowed his eyes in an effort to keep the nervous beads of sweat that were rolling from his forehead from streaming into and saturating his pupils.

"I can't believe this is happening again," he sighed. Looking to his left at the apparently unoccupied space on the backseat of the squad car, he continued, "This is all your fault. Why do you keep getting me into this shit?" He wasn't talking to himself. Well, not exactly, anyway. He was speaking to his alter ego: the dually noted, underground advice columnist and occasional influential, problem-starting connoisseur, Hottywood, of the mildly popular advice blog Ask Hottywood.

For a time, Hottywood had been brewing inside Gardner's mind until he became strong and clever enough to take full possession of him, often using the control as a means of mischief intended for the greater good of a lesser of two evils. He was the bad boy Gardner was not. He held street knowledge at his fingertips while Gardner held on tightly to lessons of the library. Hottywood was an elusive fish that always squirmed his way out of a net, leaving poor Gardner to swallow the bait and dangle on a hook until he was gutted and thrown into a hot skillet. And this fourth arrest, another notch for Hottywood in a string of fine messes, was no different from any other situation that left Gardner mad as hell.

"Sir, I didn't get you into anything. You got yourself into this. Do you realize what kind of trouble you're in?" The sound of the officer's deep raspy voice didn't match his pubescent appearance, all the while piercing through Gardner's soul like pins in a voodoo doll. He was caught off guard at the cop's response as his question wasn't directed towards him, but rather to Hottywood, who in all of his invisibility, led Gardner into yet another setup.

"You hear Officer Friendly talking to you," Hottywood teased.

"Shut up!" Gardner fired back.

"Excuse me? I don't think you are hardly in a position to break bad, Sir." The officer, looking through the rear view mirror, replied sharply.

"But I didn't…"

"I don't need to hear it, Sir. You can save your testimony until we get to the station."

A sigh from Gardner was tailed by a silent snicker from an impalpable Hottywood.

The officer aggressively shifted the gears of the squad car and pulled off, lights still flashing atop the car, accented with a shrieking siren. Gardner and his not-so-friendly arresting officer (with his invisible counter in tow) found themselves speeding down the highway in a two man, one car parade. Next stop, Rhode Island Avenue Precinct.

‡

In a secluded room in the dingy basement of a gorgeous, multi-level police headquarters, Gardner found himself handcuffed to a metal chair similar to those of an elementary school library, with only a scratched conference table and a paper cup filled with tap water for company. Beside him was an oversized, two-way mirror strategically placed for officers to watch their suspects amusingly while the suspects gazed embarrassingly into their own guilty eyes. Gardner was no exception. To him, the scene was all too familiar. The last time he was here, he faced charges for disorderly conduct at a TGI-Friday's in the flea market district of Florida Avenue, not too far from the police station where his name was seemingly becoming popular. He was arrested for walking into the restaurant's kitchen and beating a cook nearly to death with a celery stick simply for under seasoning his buffalo wings. "The voice in my head made me do it," was hardly enough to narrowly escape jail time. Thankfully, he was a praying man. It was his excessive calls to Jesus that gave pity to the sergeant responsible for locking the doors to the reserved cell blocks of the district's jailhouse.

"Let this one go," the sergeant declared. "I have a feeling he'll pay for his crimes in the prison of his own mind."

And so he did. Until this afternoon at least, when he was arrested for dropping a load of the same shit in a different toilet, barely making way to unshackled freedom . . . again.

"Mr. Gardner. Welcome back." Sergeant Sausagefoot, familiar to Gardner, greeted him with rejecting eyes and a half-hearted tone. He was a tall, bald, white man with a gray beard, a pot belly and a wrinkled Men's Warehouse suit.

"Sergeant."

"I'm going to ask you a few questions. We'll skip over the basics like 'is this your first offense?' I think we know that answer."

Gardner couldn't hide his discomfort. As chilly as it was in the room, sweat continued to pour from his forehead down to his smelly socks.

"So Mr. Gardner, it looks like you are back on the same charges you were brought in on the first three times. Let me guess. You are going to tell me that it was a voice in your head that told you to beat that kid, just like it was a voice in your head that told you to beat a restaurant worker and a Payless shoe salesman. Is that right?" Sergeant Sausagefoot's voice was unwavering. Gardner's voice, on the other hand, was full of quiver.

"Firstly, those last three charges were acquitted. Secondly, I'd like to go on record and say this is all just a big misunderstanding. I didn't beat that kid. He did." He pointed to the wall just behind him where Hottywood stood tall with a cocky smirk on his face.

"Give it up, Gardner. That's not going to work." Both Hottywood and Sergeant Sausagefoot spoke simultaneously.

This is going to be a long night, Gardner thought to himself. How the hell am I going to get out of this? Without warning he bowed his head, closed his eyes and whispered aloud an extended prayer.

Sausagefoot was set on refusal to fall prey to the sudden outbreak of the Word, but who could deny anyone a conversation with God? And so, for the next eternally long few minutes, Gardner prayed as quickly as his heart raced.

"Lord, if only you get me out of this . . ."

☦

After spending the longest ninety-five minutes ever in interrogation explaining that he has another person living inside of him that often controls his actions and an even longer stint in the commissioner's arctic office shackled to four other looming criminals, Gardner finally received his court papers and personal belongings before being escorted to his release. It was a long walk of shame, one that he'd experienced all too many times before, thanks to his blameless inner desire.

Walking down the uninviting halls of the precinct, he peered at the puke green walls. Even the bland, peeling paint was more welcoming than the obscenities scribbled along the walls of his now departed holding cell – a cell that bore an ode to him reading: GARDNER WAS HERE. AGAIN.

Once he reached the openness of outside, freedom never smelled so good. He all but fell to his knees to kiss the pavement and thank the Man upstairs for springing him from the confines of unfeeling coppers and guilty criminals. Today had marked the last day of his first life. He vowed to himself and declared openly to any passersby that would listen or could hear, to get away from Hottywood and all of the trouble that he dumped in his back pocket. This arrest, in addition to the last three, not to mention the other scenarios Hottywood has put him in over the years, was the final straw – he needed to separate himself from himself, or Hottywood, rather. Gardner was more determined than ever to be his own man – a free man. Free from the influence of the voice in his head that only he could hear. But even with that declaration, there were still a few questions that burned the back of his brain. Why was Hottywood such the troublemaker? Why did he choose Gardner to be his constant scapegoat? And lastly what time did the next bus leave town? He wanted to get as far away from Hottywood as humanly possible. You know – if Hottywood were an actual human.

Chapter 2
Face Off

I can remember the day of the arrest as if it were yesterday. All of them, actually. It was cold outside yet all I could feel was my blood boiling over from the anger of taking the fall for something I didn't do, for someone that looks like me and sounds like me and lives in me but isn't actually me. I could almost go out on a limb and say this is the story of my life, or the story of a life that isn't mine but that I live. One could argue that I speak in riddles because I'm crazy, but that isn't the case at all. I'm quite sane, actually. I was sane enough to get the hell away from the side of me that constantly leads me to trouble.

Three months ago in a land far away, I was a man with a record who lived a life synonymous with the words eccentric, daring and even fun. Today I'm kind of stuck in a rut of routine, finding myself missing the excitement that my inner brought me. Now I'm finally a practical man, boring even, if I dare say – so much so that my boldest statements are expressed through my uncanny ability of stylishly mismatching my socks; a feat not too many practical men can pull off. Don't get me wrong. I wasn't a complete prude and I'm not now. In fact, chances of finding me hanging out late on a Friday night are pretty strong, some things considered. Sure, I have a few skeletons in my closet; some that I'm proud of and some that I'm not. Who doesn't? I talk to myself sometimes. Who doesn't? Take this conversation I'm having right now for example as I sit alone in the booth of my favorite little hole-in-the wall this side of Chinatown.

☦

CLASH! From behind, a pyramid of wine goblets fall from atop a granite serving bar adorned with an antique cash register. I, along with seven other customers sitting in scattered booths across the shop, turned my head shockingly in response to the sudden shatter.

My serving host, Hector, a twenty-something-year-old, Guatemalan refugee who was adopted by the café's owners only weeks before now, excused himself from my table, incidentally after not taking my order again to sweep the glass from the floor. If I were one consumed with a little self-absorption, I would have assumed he was relieved by the calamity of the fallen dishes when my response to his routine question, "How may I help you?" resulted in a lengthy soliloquy beginning with the disclaimer, "Three months ago in a land far away, I was a man with a record who lived a life synonymous with the words eccentric, daring and even fun…"

Oddly enough, loud bangs and broken glass wasn't anything new for Graños de Café. In fact it's one of the reasons why I come here. This little drive-by dive is the only all night Asian-owned Spanish coffee shop in town that serves nothing but high end teas, and in a way, reminds me of home. Something about the sound of ambulances drag racing in the streets at all times of the night; the melodies of bullets crashing through windows and mugging victims screaming from alleyways brings it back to where it all started – back to the streets of my old neighborhood where I ran for my life from the fallout of the troubles caused by my inner conscious. Back to the good old days. The days that I secretly miss so much.

After a three month hiatus from myself, this was the perfect location to invite Hottywood back into my life to get some of my questions answered.

I moved to this city with an objective of starting a new life; a clean life; a life free from expectations and mistaken identity; a life without Hottywood, the advice guru self proclaimed to have knowledge held by the balls based on experience alone. Incidentally before I escaped his grip, I was instrumental in helping him pen his [Hottywood Helps] blog. I don't know what made me extend my help considering I was so desperate to get away from him. Truth be told, he's kind of difficult to say no to, especially when he shares the same skin as I. He's the one that many turn to for a good laugh or an unconventional idea of revenge on the company responsible for mailing to your house one advertisement too many. He's a Godsend to everyone else, but to me he's trouble dressed in fine clothes paid for with my credit card. Doctors call him my suppressed conscious. My family calls him my imagination and my friends call him my alter ego. Actually, they're all right.

Hottywood is everything I'm not. He's responsible for half of the skeletons in my closet. "The man with all the answers," is the trademark theme of the Ask Hottywood blog. However for as long as I've known him, and I've known Hottywood for a long time, he's never answered my question – "Who is Hottywood?"

As I paused to sip the remaining contents of my booze-filled mug anxiously awaiting Hector to finish spit shining the discolored café floors so he could hook me up with a refill, I turned my attention to the view beyond the dusty window pane two booths across the room. A bearded sumo wrestler impersonating a homeless, pregnant woman while begging for spare change from passersby entertained me for a while, though not without a hint of skepticism. On any given day, I'd normally throw loose change at panhandlers and run. I once got robbed by a panhandler – a sumo wrestler, believe it or not – so now when I give spare change to beggars, I literally use a long handled spoon.

Still, I feel for people that don't have much or any less than I do. Hottywood, on the other hand, would use the living image as material for his (and don't tell him I said this) hysterical weekly HORRORscopes column. I guess that's one of the differences between us. My practicality allows me to see the world through a black and white funnel while he sees the world for all its colors. I live confined within boundaries of state laws and employment contracts. He lives by self-made rules. I don't find it unimaginable to envy his loose grip on life, rules and even laws, but I've collected enough knick-knacks to have learned by now that shiny things come with a price.

Not surprisingly, our differences don't mean a hill of beans to those that believe he is nothing more than a conjure of my imagination. They simply assume my elevator is too full to reach the top floor, or as some would so eloquently put it – I'm loco. In my mind I can hear my voice urging me to be practical while competing with Hottywood's "fuck practicality" chants. All the other voices in my head are reserved for judgment and criticism. Sometimes I can't help but question my sensibility, often mistaking it for neuroticism. The truth is, if I am crazy, it's not because I have a host of voices in my head. It's because I listen to them.

Although Hottywood and I have shared the same body for what seems like my entire life, we've never been anything more than two spirits fighting for unabbreviated dominion. With time, give or take a few hits and misses, we managed to make it work. I rest with a drop of comfort knowing that while I can't get away from him, he can't function without me. I am his fingers. He is my face. Together we are the heart of Ask Hottywood. For as much as it's worth though, I still don't know what that means. But if it's the last thing I do, tonight I'm going to get into his head. I'm going to sit across from him and take a long, deep look into his eyes and dissect what therapists deem my inner desire, my split personality, my contrast, my ego. My God, where is Hector? I need another drink!

The sound of my beckoning voice sailed across the bar top and fell upon Hector's ears. No faster than a roach scurries across a kitchen counter when the lights come on was he standing before me with a pencil in one hand and a scribble pad in the other waiting patiently (as loosely as the word can be used) to take both my order and my money.

"Is there anything else I can get you, sir?"

"Sure, Hec. Do you guys have hamburgers?"

Hector responded with a look of misplaced confusion. "Of course we have hamburgers. This is a coffee shop."

"Perfect! Can I also get two rounds of the Columbian-crushed coffee bean Long Island Iced Tea?"

"Two?"

"Yeah. One for me and one for my pal."

With a raised brow, Hector looked at the empty chair sitting across the table.

"Oh no, no, no. He's not here yet. And when he does get here, you won't know because you won't see him. I'm the only one that can see him. See? But you probably don't see because all you see is me talking to me…Hector, I think I'm beginning to see your point. I'll tell you what," I continued, "Why don't you eighty-six the iced teas and just bring me the hamburger? I'll order the drinks when he gets here. Then you'll see exactly what I'm saying." I confused myself. "On another note, add an order of fries with that burger."

"Um," reluctance draped his reply. "This is a coffee shop. We don't sell fries." And with that he turned and walked away.

‡

One hamburger and fifteen minutes later, Hector had finally taken rest upon one of the bar stools, fanning away the smoke surfacing from the soles of his shoes. I turned my attention back to the performing sumo wrestler outside to update myself on his spectacle, only to fall into the glass reflection of a chocolate-skinned man with shoulder-length dreadlocks and mirrored sunshades. To no surprise, late as usual, Hottywood had come out of nowhere and rested the bum of his exorbitant "H for Hottywood" jeans in the vacant seat across the table.

"Been waiting long?" His crooked smile oozed with a confident glow bright enough for a need to wear sunshades at night.

"Long enough," I replied. "Even though you're more than thirty minutes late, I'm pretty hip to your concept of time. Here." I handed him a menu. "Look at this and pick out anything you want. Graños sells tea, tea, and tea."

"Isn't this a coffee shop?"

"What's your point?"

Hottywood's index finger vertically skimmed the menu's choices before halting to a decision.

"Hmmm. The Green Tea Baijiu looks good."

"Garçon!" I snapped my fingers to get Hector's attention, summoning him like a puppy. The wrinkles in his forehead imitated two middle fingers flipping me the bird, but I shook it off. Perhaps my misconstrued vision was a result of the effects of the liquored up tea I ingested during my wait for Hottywood's arrival. Whether I was getting on Hector's nerves or not he hurried over to the table, I had no doubt that his motivation was for nothing less than the anticipated pricey tip I was going to leave for his time and annoyance.

"What now? . . . I mean, did you want to order something else, Amigo?"

"Yes. I'll have a Green Tea Baijiu for my friend, here." With a blank expression, Hector peered once again at the empty chair then back at me.

"What's in a Green Tea Baijiu?" inquired Hottywood.

With our eyes locked on Hector, we grew speedily irritated with his muted response.

"Well?" I interjected impatiently.

"Well what?"

"Are you going to answer his question or what? I swear it's like talking to a wall," I said to Hottywood under my breath.

"Who's question?"

"Never mind, just tell us what's in a Green Tea Baijiu?"

Without goad, Hector proceeded with a description of the alcohol heavy beverage. I was impressed with his suppression of emotion. If I was him and he was me, he would surely have gotten on my nerves. Hector had clearly proven that he was well deserving of his 15% tip minus 5% for not being Jesus. Most churches only ask for 10% of one's earnings for tithes. I certainly had no intention of giving Hector more than the Man upstairs.

He mumbled something under his breath as he walked off to the kitchen. A few seconds after the swinging door closed behind him a chorus of laughter erupted among the kitchen staff. I wanted to know what the joke was most likely out of befuddled paranoia. Fortunately, I was too smashed to care that much.

"They're in there laughing at you," Hottywood said to me. A quiet giddiness followed his assumption.

"Why do you say that? I didn't do anything."

"You're fucked up. It's funny. They're laughing."

"I'm not fucked up and do you always have to be so blunt?"

"No, but I'll take one if you have it," he retorted.

Here we go, I thought to myself. Hottywood and I can't be in a room for more than two minutes without colliding.

"Look H-wood, I didn't call you here to argue. I asked you to come because I want to talk to you."

"About?"

"About you."

"What about me?"

"I want to know who Hottywood is."

"Um, whatchu talkin' 'bout? You know better than anyone who Hottywood is."

I couldn't understand why but he seemed almost offended by my question.

"Not quite," I tried to explain. "I know who you are in theory, but I don't know who you are. I don't know anything about you except how you think. What drives you? What makes you Hottywood? For as long as I've known you I have no idea about the life you live when we're not together. Every memory, every experience that I have is of us; of you steering me into some kind of trouble that I'm barely able to get out of. I want to step away from dictating blogs for a minute to hear the story of Hottywood as told by you. It's like that old saying goes, "Go straight to the ass.""

"You mean 'straight from the horse's mouth'?"

This time it was my turn to squelch a chuckle across the table. "Yeah, what you said."

We sat there a while longer trading barbs at one another. Our quips reminded me of as many good days with my concealed counterpart almost as much as my nuisance reasons for running away from him. As often as Hottywood and I bickered, our rivalry was more a term of endearment than anything else.

Our offset balance oscillated between right and wrong and sometimes good and evil. For the most part, our symmetry panned out. His carefree spirit allowed me a privilege to live on the edge. Something I did not ordinarily do without reading the fine print on the repercussions of the adventure. My reasonableness allowed him to keep on living without getting the crap beaten out of him. I'd have to say though, I think our contrast is what makes our bitter sweet relationship so special, not to mention sets the tone for and makes Ask Hottywood work. My common sense when combined with his lack thereof makes for a perfect "tell it like it is", one-stop shop for problem solving for those persons in need of guidance, which again brings us full circle to why we're here.

"Hector!" I called out. "Another round for the table, if you will. It looks like this is going to be a long night."

While rolling his eyes in the back of his head, Hector whipped up the Asian herbs that make Graños de Café's Spanish teas unmatched by any other coffee shop competitor. I really didn't want another drink. I was afraid one more sip would have me passed out under the table. I figured Hottywood could use another, and I couldn't let him outdo me.

Still, everyone knows diarrhea of the mouth is inevitable when one has had one drink too many beyond the normal capacity for the average man, though Hottywood, the self-promulgated know-it-all is no average man.

I propped my back against the rest of my cushioned seat, staring at myself through the reflective lenses of Hottywood's aviator shades. An ensemble of violins played softly in the background as he began his tale. It was nice for a change to hear his voice speak to me from outside my head. His words flowed like a poet. He had my undivided attention.

"You and I," he began, "are really not that different. One of my favorite writers…me," he joked. "…once said 'we all possess a voice as unique as our fingertips.' I am who I am as a result of the influences of the world and the people in it, even the people I don't know and the situations I've not directly been in the middle of. I've been fascinated by people and the relationships they have with their emotions for as long as I can remember. Growing up as an only child, people-watching was often more amusing than instigating wars between my G.I. Joe action figures. My story is one that's ongoing and one I've not been able to share, which is where you come in. I need someone sensible enough to tell the story. And let's face it, I'm intangible and you're kind of a dud. You need me so you can have some stories to tell at parties. We can't advise people on things we haven't experienced. So now that I think about it, I'm glad you asked who Hottywood is. It's time for you to take a walk in my shoes."

Chapter 3

Who is Hottywood?

Who am I? I am a holiday miracle born two months behind schedule. I am a page taken from stories of experiences shared by many, told through my eyes. I am a hybrid of both good and evil, a line drawn between right and wrong. I am reason. I am purpose. I am an extension of preceding generations and a plow for those that follow. I am laughter in the midst of sadness and hurt and long lines at the grocery store. I am one without regret. I am.

I am the faint voice in your head that chuckles at all the dumb stuff happening around you, including the things no one else has the kahunas to find funny. I am an imaginary friend only seen by those who believe in the powerful healing of humor. I am what a french fry is to a burger. What peanut butter is to jelly. What sugar is to Kool Aid. I am necessary. I am.

I am the angel that sits on your right shoulder, steering you from wrong; and the devil that sits on your left, aiming rubber bands at the right when wrongful consequence serves a more valuable purpose. I am light. I am darkness. I am not always right, but I am never wrong. I am.

I am a life guide to all, a north star to most, refreshing to many, a love to some, an acquaintance to few, a friend to fewer, and a mystery to the remaining. I. Am. Hottywood.

A long time ago, I accepted a responsibility delivered to me through a ray of light shining from above to show others that silly nuisances are fortuitous climaxes that fill one's drama between plot and purpose. I was deemed by the heavens to be a run on sentence for a reason of how and why "shit happens." My wisdom cannot be justified without explaining how I came to be.

This is the story of how a small town boy from a little village in a big city became a supplemental name when worry dried out all vocabulary of profanity. This is my story. Welcome to Hottywood.

☦

The night was cruel. Cold air cried frozen tears upon DC's slippery streets. The stars winked at the moon. The dark skies glowed with a snowy light. From below, life was still. No movement. No breath. From the inside of a Southeast Community Hospital maternity ward window, high above pavements dressed in sheets of ice, a beautiful young girl was about to give birth to an angelic baby boy. In all of the eighteen years and nine months that she dodged the bullets of trials and error of youth, she was about to experience her life change within a second of time's touch.

Releasing controlled short breaths in sets of four, her eyes closed tightly, she saw moments of her life sail across her mind. She won her first spelling bee when she was in the fourth grade. By the end of her middle school year, she was voted most popular student. After becoming captain of the cheerleading team in her senior year of high school, she was elected student body president. She also, as luck had it, found love.

His name was Charles Who. As a quarterback on the field and point guard on the court, Charles was himself, a school trophy. Good looking, athletic, and popular, he was quite the catch. Every girl pined over him, much to the dismay of many. As worthless as a bag of rocks, Charles treated his girlfriends in equal value changing them as often as he changed his socks until he stumbled upon one girl that possessed a quality like no other girl in the school. They were perfect together. The jock and the miss congeniality were quickly tagged an "it" couple. To her, he was the love of her life. To him, she was the only girl worthy to stand beside him as his prom queen. The sweethearts dated from the second semester of their senior year until four months after their graduation.

Holding true to his reputation, Charles disposed of the relationship when he fell smitten with another blossoming social flower. In a matter of a few short months, the beautiful young girl felt the sting of a broken heart and the betrayal of an absentee father to her unborn child. She was sad at first, afraid of being a single mother scorned by love, and heavily burdened with doubt. But in the forty-ninth minute of the late tenth hour on that cold February night, all of her fears went away when, after nine months of carrying a legacy in her uterus, she gave birth to a handsome baby boy. Five months after the breakup with the love of her life, she had fallen in love for the first time again. That beautiful young girl once full of questions that began with "Why?" had stepped into the role of mother – my mother – a woman who now holds all the answers that begins with "Because."

From the moment she brought me home, she raised me with care. She was my mother first, my father second, and finally, my friend. Mama brought me up in the heart of church and family. She raised me to be obedient, respectful, chivalrous, and observant. She taught me to do right and steer clear from the path of evil. In so doing, she kept me in a circle of like minded church going friends – friends that were great and who I loved very much, even though I desperately wanted to escape the dynamics of church.

To me, church folk were one dimensional, even the kids. With church being just a few steps away from home, my perception of a broad world extended no further than the distance between my bedroom window and the storefront sanctuary up the block. Just as sure as I knew the world wasn't flat, I knew there was more to life beyond the street lights of my quaint little neighborhood. There had to be.

Like my mother in her prime, I was popular. I wasn't quite as meticulous with my studies as she once was, but I tasted every extracurricular activity I could sink my teeth into. The activities exposed me to worlds only written in pages, and quenched my thirst for social diversity. Popularity was as important as good grades, much to no surprise for a grade school student. Being held in high regard by my peers warranted a reward higher in value than braving a month's punishment for bringing home an "F" on my report card. The lyrics of my song rang familiar to Mama's ears, particularly remaindering her of when Charles Who fronted her list of priorities, trumping academics and clear judgment. Mentally recapping her childhood, she saw a replication of herself in me. Proudly, she saw respect, determination, and charisma. Contemptuously, she saw naiveté, rebellion, and stubbornness. When stirred all together, whether with a finger or a spoon, it served up one nasty potion. Worry was Mama's shower cap. I watched every day as her shiny black tresses slowly turned silver, unaware that I was the dye that stripped her hair gray. Time set a repeat of history into motion on the night I was born. She, before my arrival, yearned for a life that would today only be glamorized on reality television. Like most underrated series, her season was short lived. Her closeups were few except on blooper reels, and her happy endings rarely ended with a laugh track. Bitterly sweet, she watched closely as I found solace in my own skin, silently weary of my susceptibility of making a single ill-advised decision, much like her faux relationship with Charles Who that could one day change my life forever. I was her, revised. Part two. Roll tape.

Mama's worry about me didn't have as much to do with popularity as she thought, though at that young age it wasn't quite so simple to convince her of that. It was more about me identifying with people who had just as many questions as I. Identifying with people on a quest to identify with themselves, just as I. I was eager to travel all the roads that led me from a young boy wishing he were grown to a young man wishing to turn back the clock. I was ready to cruise big streets and digest billboards of all things restricted to anyone under eighteen, namely myself. Mama had driven the same streets as I until she hit a bump that left her permanently parked.

Growing up as an only child, I easily found entertainment in all things around me. I made Kool Aid popsicles. Music was my comfort. I penned my deepest thoughts in soul soothing poetic prose. No matter how much I earned or was given, it was never enough. People were my true infatuation, arguably because the roaches under my bed couldn't engage in conversation. It was the personalities of others that attracted me, even when those personalities smelled like a fat kid's underarms after gym class. Their moods turned me both on and off. Their intentions intrigued me. It wasn't long before I began to flirt with my attraction to those brought up beyond walls familiar and opposite my own, outside of my home and my church.

At school, I didn't hang with a particular group of people. I thought that to be a limitation on what I could gain from others. Instead I hung with everyone, those high on the totem pole, and those not so much. I watched the stapled cliques and how they interacted with one another – the geeks, the diva and her minions, the populars, the honorable mentions, and those without a niche. They all mimicked battling villages of small tribes, secluding themselves in respective sections of a jungle. When they met it was a spectacle. The geeks were geniuses, but not smart enough to dominate the populars. Everyone got cavities whenever the diva walked into the room. Her shit didn't stink. The populars set the trends. Where they led, everyone followed. The honorable mentions walked a borderline of here today, gone tomorrow. Luck allowed them to skate by with the populars, although as fickle as luck was then (and is now) it was unsurprising if they fell into a trench of those without a niche. Fast forwarding some years later, those tribes find themselves now unclear on where they rank among society, love, wealth, and even worth.

Today, the old school geeks (still shunned by those that wear clothes expensively tagged with the names of someone other than their own) run companies that drain the bank accounts of the former populars, divas, and honorable mentions. They reign supreme in the realm of business, yet fall beneath the cornerstone of visible popularity. They dominate the business's books, but their little black books are as empty as their beds.

The diva that once filled the school halls with scents of rose buds is still as beautiful as her yearbook picture, if in fact you are looking at her yearbook picture. Today, her ass wraps around her waist twice, her breasts are transported in a wheel barrel, and she throws her troubles to the bottom of a two-liter root beer bottle. She no longer questions what she's going to wear to the next big event. Instead, she questions why she wasn't invited.

Within a few exhales of time's breath, the lives of the members of those cliques changed as quickly as did the life of the beautiful young girl that gave birth to a little bundle of joy thirty-six years ago. And like that young girl, each member of those tribes – the geeks, the divas, the populars, the honorable mentions, and those without a niche – have me. Only now I have clothed my real life experiences – love gained and love lost – with festive wrapping paper to give to those with dull revelations, just as my mother had once given me before the law of the land took precedence over the wisdom of motherhood.

I am because I have accepted my place in this world to carry out a legacy of rationale for those that have lost their way. In the hope of saving if only but one from the embarrassment of an unnecessary hardship, relationship, or pink slip, I have pledged to be a tour guide for questionability.

My advice is more than just that. It is a journey. It is a reason for my reasoning. It is an answer of wisdom, the kind of wisdom your mother didn't give you and the kind of wisdom only experience can teach.

☦

The busyness of the café had become almost silent. The spectacles outside ceased. Hector rested on a bar stool a few feet away from Hottywood and I. The clanking of stirring spoons banging against coffee cups emulated a cymbal section of an orchestra. It was the perfect setting for a storytelling.

For some reason, at that very moment, I felt as if I were speaking to Hottywood for the first time. Without actually removing his shades, he'd taken them off and allowed me a chance to look into the windows of his soul. As he walked me down a path of his life I was beginning to piece together a reason for his being. He was longing to understand people and why they behave the way they do. Perhaps it was too soon to tell why he behaved the way he did and used me as a shield from stray bullets, but oddly I found slight satisfaction in knowing that his behavior was not without purpose and, even more, not coated in sole malice.

  I took a barbaric bite of my burger and washed it down with a swig from the contents of my mug, pretending I was feasting on a tub of buttered popcorn and a giant cup of soda as he continued with his chronicle. I didn't know exactly where he was going with it, but it sounded like it was off to a good start.

Chapter 4

The Birds and the Bees

My path to the independent study of people began a few short weeks after the incident where the Miracle Gro that I rubbed on my chest burned off the new growth rather than the intended opposite. Against the will of my mother, experience and observation became my teacher. I broke the bubble of family ties and church, and made the streets my playground. I had become seemingly reckless to anyone that wasn't me. I played with fire to discover for myself just how much it burned. I got punched in the face twice before understanding that the term "turn the other cheek" was just an expression. Basically, I was a stupid kid that insisted on breaking a few rules in order to understand why rules weren't meant to be broken. And then came love. It didn't take my heart to get broken to become familiar with the hurt of loss. At least not right away. Instead, thanks to a dense fog of friendship with four quirky characters, I became an expert in the meaning behind the story of the birds and the bees.

It all began in a courtyard of single family row houses on the south side of Fairfax Village and Alabama Avenue in Washington, DC. Michael Domack, my best friend and the Village's resident funny man, lived in the corner house just beyond the entrance of the courtyard. He was the youngest of six brothers and probably the only one of them with any common sense. All of his brothers lived at home with their mother and alleged father, but spent most of their time on the street selling weed to save up enough money to buy a van that any one of them could crash in when one of the parents kicked them out of the house for the night. Unfortunately, they were so busy smoking their merchandise that the only time they saw the inside of a van was when they were being hauled off in a paddy wagon by a SWAT team of cops.

It was never difficult for Michael to come up with funny material. He lived it every day. With a mother who could have been a recurring guest on the Maury Povich show, a syndicated American tabloid talk show that deals with a variety of issues heavily focusing on sexual infidelity and paternity test results, a father that only came home when he couldn't bum $0.50 from passersby at the bus stop, and five brothers that were probably made girlfriends at one point or another in a 7th district cell block, he cracked jokes to deflect possible insults lashed at him by all of the other neighborhood kids. Fortunately, he was so witty that he never had any problems out of anyone. Although his wit was incomparable, a small part of me thinks no one bothered him because his family was screwed up enough to beat the hell out of anyone that spoke sideways about their lifestyle: Yet another reason why he was my friend and not my enemy.

Michael and I met in grade school. From the moment we met, we clicked. He was funny as all outdoors and I was silly enough to laugh at all of his jokes. Together, we never had a dull moment. I guess you can say he was the brother I never had and I was the brother he always wanted – you know, because his biological brothers weren't shit. We experienced a lot together. We accidentally killed our classroom pet frog, Mr. Plagelmeyer. We were the first to throw stink bombs in the school cafeteria so the administration would be forced to close the lunch room and institute an impromptu pizza party for the whole school. We skipped classes together. Not all of them, only the ones we were failing. We stole a car once. That didn't go very well because neither of us knew how to drive. My ass still hurts from when my mother whooped me with an extension cord for both stealing and getting caught. That was perhaps the day I vowed never to get caught in an intentional wrongdoing again, or at least have in reserve a wingman dumb enough to take the blame.

Then, hormones kicked in. Enter the Bagumgum twins, Marlene "Bird" Bagumgum and her sister, Marlecka "Bee". Bird and Bee were the most sought after girls in the neighborhood, each for different reasons. Bird, the quietest of the twins, was known for her charm. She was a lady, a real class act. People respected her because she commanded respect without being demanding about it. To call her an introvert would be a bit of a stretch. She knew how to get attention and she loved to get it, though she never had to try hard unlike her sister, Bee, who was a walking bull horn. You could hear Bee coming down the street before she stepped foot on the block. If it wasn't her loud mouth, it was the click clack of her four inch wooden wedges that let out a distress signal when she stepped on the scene. Bee was feisty. She was a purely confident hood chick in the truest sense. Bamboo earrings, tight miniskirts and a man for every day of the week was her M.O. As long as whatever wiener she roasted had enough money to keep her decked out in the flashiest name brand knockoff gear. She was a black Madonna; a material girl, and probably the first gold digger I'd ever met.

The other girls around the way couldn't take either one of them. They were jealous of Bird because she was an innocent good girl that got what she wanted simply by being herself. They hated Bee because she thought she was "all that." They hated her even more because all the dudes around the way also thought she was all that and Bee cleverly used that to her advantage. While Bird used her personality to win over a crowd, Bee used her feminine wilds, often times stealing some other broad's man. The fist brawls between Bee and the neighborhood chicks were epic, more so when Bird came to her defense. Bird didn't like confrontation, but she didn't let anyone fuck with her sister, even when Bee was in the wrong.

I took particular interest in the twins, not only because they were fine but because their differences afforded me an opportunity to fully understand the birds and the bees in relation to the approach to sexual social behavior. My mother tried to explain the traditional story of the birds and the bees to me but I didn't know what the hell she was talking about. I don't think she knew what the hell she was talking about. At any rate, the similarity between the Bagumgums' approach to sexual behavior and the story of the birds and the bees, as I can recall, were freakishly analogous. The similiarity however didn't become evident until our circle closed with its final member, Willy Shahoolahoop. Yes, that was his real name – Shahoolahoop.

Willy and Michael were longtime friends brought up together in his grandmother's church. They knew each other probably longer than Michael and I. Around the time when everyone rocked fat 24k gold-dipped rope chains and Sergio Tacchini sweat suits, Willy moved in with his grandmother who lived on the edge of the Village. His parents were big time dope dealers that got caught up in a highly publicized sting raid. The cops busted in on them one night, seized them, their immediate accomplices, butt loads of cash, and enough evidence to send them to jail for the next few presidential terms. They sent Willy along with an undisclosed amount of money (rumor had it) to his sweet old apple pie baking, gun toting grandmother whom everyone loved and was afraid to cross. Her home's curbside appeal was decked out with lavish double breasted suit wearing storefront church pastors and hooligans that wore bandanas around their heads and drove black cars with even blacker windows. Willy's grandma wasn't to be messed with because she was protected by agents of both God and the devil.

Willy introduced to the neighborhood kids a trendy style inclusive of large sums of $1 bills rolled up in thick bundles. He stapled the look of a six figure making hip-hopster. He was no doubt the first perpetrator I'd ever met. Maybe that's why I never liked him. He was a show off and nobody likes a showoff. And by nobody I mean me.

His upgraded B-Boy style left a remarkable impression on almost everyone, including Bee, and excluding myself and Bird. All of the attention quickly went to his head. In no time at all, his egotism morphed into a no grade braggadocio. He invested a lot of time bragging over where he rested on the social ladder. It was pretty annoying. Sometimes in my head, I would pretend he was rocket-launched into a freak meteor shower. Hearing him scream in terror would have been more entertaining than hearing him constantly put the "I" in "team." Given Bird's facial expressions in response to Willy's every word, coupled with her noticeably painful implosions, her dislike for Willy was as strong as mine. Unfortunately, as rapidly as Willy's head grew, so did Bee's eyes, which put a damper on Bird's negative feelings towards him. Green wads and nice clothes were Bee's Achilles' heel and the two qualities she found most attractive in men. Because of that, Bird had to be her sister's keeper.

A couple of weeks passed, giving everyone time to adjust to Willy's arrival and ego. He rode the coat tails of his newly acquired popularity like kids ride roller coasters, bringing along Michael (his best friend and sidekick), me (the sidekick understudy "affiliated by association" Willy's words, not mine), and, ironically (or not), the twins. Bee followed Willy everywhere he went. She was careful to hide behind shadows like a ninja warrior focused on the stillness of a clean kill. Quietly, she watched his every move, displaying an inaudible side that no one deemed physically possible for this usually vivacious whippersnapper. Willy's skill at maneuvering through hoards of ghetto girls clad in second skin bleached jeans with blank child support checks duct taped to their back pockets was as precise as Bee's ability to reduce a man's cool points by dollar signs rather than numbers. She wasn't merely intrigued by his undeniable notoriety. She was attracted to the audacity of him not booking her first.

It was amazing to watch her in action. She buzzed around Willy like an annoying little yellow jacket. As subtle as she was (as well as sometimes purposely obvious), no matter if or how much anyone swatted, she wouldn't fly away. After a while, she became as cute as the little bee on all the Cheerios commercials. Just like those commercials, she interjected thirty second advertisement plugs for her honey oats to Willy. Girlfriend was hot in the pants. I almost needed a bucket of popcorn when she turned on the theatrics. Watching her throw herself at him was like watching a week ending soap opera building to a climax that often ended with a breath clenching, cliff hanging commercial break. Bee's performances always left us with something to laugh about. I laughed because I never knew if she was going to speak through her mouth or her vagina. Willy laughed because whenever Bee wasn't around, he'd quip about how he was going to tap that ass. Bird, being the devoted sister that she was, always stood close by Bee's side. She poured her embarrassment into a cup and mixed in a lemon flavored packet of giggles, which, when stirred with Michael's on the spot stand up punch lines, created a cup of bitter sweet amusement at Bee's expense that rivaled the flavor of a cherry smash soda. As Bee's spectacles continued, so did the amount of time the five of us spent together. In that way, we all sort of started hanging out and soon became friends. This is when my first lesson in love began. Also, quite possibly, the first time I tried my hand at mischievous mayhem at the expense of another.

   Although Willy and Michael were close, and Bee was up Willy's ass for all the wrong reasons, Bird and I still thought Willy was a filthy dog that smelled fishy. Still, out of my respect for the relationship between him and Michael, and Bird's respect for Bee's process of pollination, we tolerated him. Trust me. Tolerating Willy was no easy feat. To describe the toleration was synonymous to eating a sour pickle for the first time and realizing that you are allergic to pickles, and all of a sudden your tongue swells, your throat closes, and your taste buds pop off one bud at a time. In contrast, in all the time that we spent crossing off items from the "Why We Hate Willy" list, Michael spent an equal amount of time shifting his assiduity to Bird, who received his attention with warm welcome, ultimately changing the dynamic of our already unstable out of the box circle.

It wasn't long after I noticed both twins pining over Michael and Willy that I realized just how different the sisters were. A couple of house parties later, Bird and Bee finally found themselves locked into relationships with their sought after suitors, leaving me to be the fifth wheel of the bunch, and the only one that didn't make an ass out of myself.

Bird and Michael gradually progressed into their relationship. They did the whole "Can I have a chance? Check 'yes' or 'no,'" thing. Bee and Willy, on the other hand, fell into their relationship behind a Dominos pizza joint on the main avenue as they dry humped each other against a dirty, oversized trash dumpster.

Dear Hottywood,

I've been hollering at this girl for the last two weeks. The positive is that she's a nice and pretty girl. The negative is that since we've been talking, all she talks about is sex. Naturally, I want to hit it, but contrary to what she thinks (or wants) I have more to offer than just dick. In theory, she could very well be "the one," but I never thought I had to mould my soul mate. That isn't gay or anything is it?

After Hours

Dear After Hours,

Not wanting to discuss sex with this chick (or anyone, for that matter) 24/7 doesn't make you gay. It makes you mature. To be quite honest with you, it's refreshing to hear from a dude with more than just pussy on his mind.

I'm not going to tell you that this broad isn't the perfect one for you, but if you're in doubt after fourteen days, chances are you aren't too far off the mark. After all, men [and women] know when they've met the one after the first date…even more commonly after the first fifteen minutes of conversation.

You can either tell her how you feel and give her a chance to discover another kind of conversation other than what she picked up from old Vanessa Del Rio movies, or you can bone her and move on. Be warned that if you choose door #2, and the sex turns out to be as good as she anticipates, you will have a whole other problem on your hands. So, it's probably best that you have a sit down with her and tell it like it is. As long as she continues to wear her vagina on her sleeve, chances are she's going to have this same problem with the next man in her life. And it's most likely that the next man won't have his morals in check like you seemingly do.

If you don't feel like wasting your breath explaining to her that there's more to life than lube, rubbers or raw boning, screw her and leave $20 on the nightstand after the deed is done. Maybe she'll feel cheap enough to re-evaluate her whorish ways. You will have gotten some ass and (presumably, if she doesn't like the emotionless treatment) she'll feel too used to call you again. It's a win/win for you, provided that she doesn't pass some kind of an STD on. That's the chance you'll take for following the instinct of the head in your pants instead of the one on your shoulders.

"While you are free to choose your own action

Consequences come with a price."

Fairly quickly, the dust settled on the newness of the relationships between Michael, Willy, and the twins. Things were going smoothly for a while. Admittedly, I found some discomfort with being sandwiched between two couples, but by the time I'd gotten use to the idea, the novelty had worn off. Michael and Bird quickly became the "it" couple of the block, while Willy and Bee took on an emulation of a tumultuous Ike and Tina Turner. It should not go unsaid that neither relationship came without problems. Michael's hormones were out of control every time Bird came around. Equally, so were hers. Whenever the two got together, their bodies stuck together like refrigerator magnets. It was like watching soft porn in 3-D. They kissed a lot. And by a lot, I mean get a room. It was easy to assume they were boning each other in somebody's basement when nobody's parents were home. Sadly, that was not the case. As much as Michael wooed Bird with his charm, she was holding on to a little secret that she only shared with her sister, until the night of the red light party at Willy's house.

Everyone who was anyone was there. Guys and gals grinded on each other in the middle of a dark, low ceiling basement while Boyz II Men's "Uhh Ahh – The Sequel" played on the boom box. The punch bowl was spiked with vodka miniatures and everyone that wasn't immediately on the floor grooving to the smooth tunes of the song's final chorus was eyeballing the he or she next to be pulled to the dance floor with the succeeding slow jam. Some people flirted with each other. Others stamped their claim with love bites. Michael and Bird were no exception. He found himself holed up in a corner of the room with his tongue wrapped around Bird's tonsils. You would have thought they were in the room all by themselves the way they carried on. No one minded though, partly because everyone was horny little teenagers just waiting to do the grown up. The steam in that room could have been cut with a butter knife. The stench was stronger than onion pizza and baby oil. Before long, Michael and Bird slipped into a walk-in coat closet.

Three flights up on the second floor of the house, Bee and Willy gyrated all over their naked bodies behind the locked doors of his bedroom. They were careful not to make any noise that disturbed his grandmother, although she knew that Willy, like his parents, was a bit of a wild child. Grandma preferred him to do his dirt at home under her supervision. She had already lost Willy's parents to the streets. She didn't want to lose him the same way. Willy didn't care much of what his grandmother thought. Actually, he didn't care much of what anyone thought. He just didn't want to disrespect her in her own home. As much of an asshole as he was, he did manage to salvage enough decency to maintain a certain amount of respect for his elders, only not so much to not fuck in her house.

Meanwhile, downstairs in the coat closet, Bird stepped outside of her character. She licked and kissed Michael in places he only fantasized about. His hands stayed stuck to her breasts and buns as if they were applied with extra strength envelope glue. Things got hot, heavy, and loud. On the other side of the closet door, me and just about every other party guest had our ears tuned as moans echoed from the other side. Bird's exclamations overrode the music of the boom box, heating everyone up in ways no one was experienced enough to understand. Shortly after, gratifying moans turned into escalated muffled words.

"Wait…wait. Stop. We…we can't. Michael, we can't do this." Bird's words were broken into short breaths as she fought off Michael's stronghold. She wanted him desperately, but was apprehensive about unlocking the padlock she had clamped to her va-jeezy.

Michael was not happy. "Come on, baby. Don't stop now. Let me just put the head in."

Forget what was happening on the dance floor. Everyone was interested in what was happening inside that closet.

"Michael, STOP!" She pushed him off of her, shoving him hard enough to thump against the wall.

"Why are you bullshitting?" Michael quickly changed his tone, frustrated with Bird for getting him all worked up for nothing.

I sprung into action to get everyone to back away from the door and out of their business. I wasn't as concerned with what was happening inside the closet because I knew I was going to get the 411 first hand anyway. Still, I wanted the door all to myself so I could hear as much as I could before I received an official update.

"Michael," Bird responded. "We just can't do this."

"What do you mean we can't do this? Why not?"

"We're in a closet with a room full of people on the other side of that door. I don't want my first time to be like this." There was a sincerity in her voice that rubbed Michael's back lovingly.

"Your first time? You mean?"

"Yes," she interrupted. "I'm a virgin. I may look like my sister but I'm not her."

"Baby I'm sorry." Michael felt like a heel, still simmering.

"There's more."

He braced himself for the news next to come.

"I'm saving myself for marriage."

"Ah, hell no!" I blurted. My eyes and nose squinted and I threw my hands to the air. "Damn! Damn! Damn!" I felt Michael's pain and I wasn't even getting any.

Everyone's jaws dropped. If no one knew for sure what was going on before Bird's confession, we all sure as hell knew nothing was going to happen after it. I could only imagine the look on Michael's face. At the age of a number that ended in the letters t-e-e-n, marriage was the last thing on his mind.

Dear Hottywood,

My boo just got her hair done and now she won't let me have sex with her. How long is long enough to wait?

Hard Up

Dear Hard Up,

You might as well join the ranks of great men far and wide that have been shot down by women with freshly done hairdos. That's like a woman asking a man to have sex during the Super Bowl. Women are shallow when it comes to their hair. And one thing's for certain, there is no way on God's green earth that she is going to let you ruin it right after it's been freshly done.

If I were you, I'd wait about three to five days before trying to lay the pipe – depending on how well the 'do holds up. In the course of those three to five days, your "boo" will probably sleep standing up like a horse. She will not leap. She will not run. She will probably glide on roller skates before her feet touch the ground. Too much movement causes one to sweat, which is like kryptonite to a woman's hair, hence your dilemma. Sorry, Charlie. Other than ice cubes and cold showers, porno will be your concubine for the next few days.

You can speed up the process, but it may cost you. If you take her out for a night on the town, she may repay you by taking you to second base. If you can afford to have her kitchen remodeled by a beautician, your chances of getting some cupcakes will be even better. If you have a voice of gold and can sing her panties into a bunch, you might be able to get some. But if you can sing and have a negative bank account or a zero balance on your prepaid credit card, you'd better save that ammo for your last resort.

For the sake of your pride, use this time to make love to her mind. If you make love to her mind the chances of going a few flights lower will be in your favor. In the end, though, your patience will achieve more than begging. Puppy dog eyes only work for puppies. I feel your pain and I wish you luck.

"Potato chips will give you the same comfort as rebound sex . . .

    If you are over a thousand pounds and have never experienced sex."

The tides shifted after the party. Bird and Michael went to great lengths to avoid one another. Or rather Michael went to great lengths to avoid Bird. Not because Bird refused to give it up, but because she kept such a huge secret from him. He didn't know what other secrets she could be keeping, which led him to settle uncomfortably in the notion that there was something more important she wasn't sharing with him, her trust. His heart was more damaged than his ego. The only way he knew how to process the after party was to put on the cloak of absence, which prior to my expertise in advising people with better judgment, was probably my fault. I may have suggested that he didn't want to waste his time with a chick that wasn't trying to give up any booty, especially when he'd come so close. I had my nerve though, being the only single person in our group. But I didn't know any better and obviously neither did Michael. He listened to me. Yet another reason why we were friends.

Distance proved to be more difficult than either of us expected. There was still the matter of Bee and Willy. Where Willy was, there was Bee. Where there was Bee, there was Bird. Michael couldn't get away from Bird because she hung with her sister, who followed Willy, who rolled tight with Michael and me. Our broken wheel kept spinning in the same circle.

The disconnect between Michael and Bird didn't have an effect on Willy and Bee. Their relationship was based on something more tangible than emotion. Willy's version of classroom share time was way different from Michael's. He was more of a kiss and tell kind of guy. Willy boasted about his conquests. He told the whens, wheres, and hows, proving that men, too, gossip. He never once described any moment with Bee using words that defined something you could not physically feel. Bee was just another number in his phone book. Word on the street was Willy was hooking up with some other girls – Keysha, Boosie, and some chick that didn't warrant a strong enough impression to remember her name. They didn't live in the Village with us, but DC is a small town and Willy never shied away from running his mouth. Neither did I. And I didn't like Willy anyway, so…

Naturally, being his friends, or in my case acquaintance, Michael and I knew the rumors were true, but we played the "dumb" card when we had to. Admittedly, I was playing the dumb card to cover my own ass for spreading his business, but that's another story. As it turned out, we really didn't have to keep any secrets at all. Willy was the one that put the word on the street in a bitter sweet attempt to boost his own celebrity. What he didn't know was that the last time he and Bee had sex on the back of a moped, she lo-jacked his balls. While he was out sneaking around with Keysha, Boosie and that other chick, she had already gotten the word off the street before he had a chance to put it out there himself. He made himself look like a fool and I didn't have to do a damn thing but sit back and gloat. He made himself my wingman, stuck with my blame of spreading the word of his own mess.

‡

Bee was no rookie. She was a bad bitch. She had dudes folded up in the bottom of her coach bag. Any fellow that took a deep, long look into her nonprescription, hazel brown contact lenses instantly fell under her spell. She had a man for everything she wanted – money, shoes, McDonald's, home pregnancy tests – you name it. But Bee plotted to get next to Willy. Her steps were not ordered by nature as Bird's were to Michael. She studied him. She knew everything about him from the time he woke up in the morning until the time he took his last dump at night. There was something she wanted from him that warranted that kind of effort. Since

Willy was as much of a glutton for ass as she was for the material, they were a match made in train wreck heaven. You had to admire their tenacity.

Dear Hottywood,

I broke into my boyfriend's voicemail and found the number of the girl he's been cheating with. What should I say when I call her?

Red-Handed

Dear Red-Handed,

It was either a wise man or a spider that once said, "Oh what a tangled web we weave when first we practice to deceive."

You should be ashamed of yourself for breaking into your boyfriend's phone. Therein lies your problem. A whole bunch of things suddenly come to mind: lack of trust, karma, that whole "eye for an eye/tooth for a tooth" thing. By hacking into his phone, which is a violation of privacy and I'm sure some kind of law, you placed an unnecessary stress on yourself, and have opened a door for a potential restraining order. If you had a reason to think he was cheating on you, then you should have been packing your bags to go home to mother, away from your cheating lover. Instead, you chose a route that led you to an equal standpoint of untrustworthiness.

Before you think about approaching anyone with anything, you need to have a reasonably acceptable answer to give when your man questions your rights of being a snoop. Nosiness is the eighth of the seven deadly sins. Once you've dusted your boots on those grounds, you should keep in mind that your troubles do not fall on some third party, but rather on you and your beau alone. Calling the other woman will merely add to your stress. She should be the last thing on your mind, the first thing being the question of what's left [in your relationship] if you have no trust.

I'm not going to tell you that you and this guy shouldn't or can't be together. And I'm not going to tell you that the girl he's cheating with doesn't need to have her ass kicked. What I am going to tell you is that you need to focus on making yourself your number one priority, learn how to pick and choose your battles and when to walk away, sans a restraining order, keeping in mind that few men walk away from battles without scars. For a time, chase dreams. Not people.

Everyone gathered at the community recreation center, Hype for Less. It also quadrupled as a bowling alley, a delicatessen, a laundromat, and a support center for people that hate cats and fast food. Michael and I sat in lane six of the bowling alley, close to the french fry bar – another one of my brilliant suggestions, thanks to the fat kid in me. Willy, as weird as he was, hung out in the laundromat. He got a kick out of watching women fold their panties fresh out of the dryer. Bird, dressed in a matching outfit with her sister, posted herself at the entrance of the center. This afforded her a direct line of eye contact between the bowling alley, where Michael was, and the drop off point in front of the building where Bee could be seen bent over with her head inside one of the black cars that frequented Willy's home front.

  Michael, since his episode with Bird, wasn't the same. He was withdrawn and lackluster, which for Michael was out of the ordinary. In all our conversations he tried hard not to bring up Bird's name. Being apart from her was tearing him up. I couldn't help but feel guilty for encouraging him to stay away from her. Perhaps that encouragement was my first experience of hating? Either way I missed having Bird around myself. Not only was she the light that shined inside my best friend, she was the only person that appreciated my revulsion of Willy. And anyone that hated Willy as much as I did deserved to hang around me so we could badmouth him together.

Willy finally tore himself away from the laundromat, as the last woman in the facility folded her final unmentionable. His satisfied smile entered the vestibule before the rest of him, greeting Bird at the front door.

"What's up B? Where's your sister?"

Bird was a little nervous. She knew her sister was up to no good, but as always protected her by any means necessary. She could have chilled wine as cool as she remained.

"Oh, she's hanging around somewhere." She sized him up. "Willy, you're looking good today. Check you out! I can see why my sister is all up in your grill. Come on. Buy me something to eat? We can hang out at the fry bar until Bee gets here."

Before Bird could fully intertwine her arm with his to lead him away, Willy managed to steal a look outside of the building only to spot Bee's backside waving to him. He made no mention of it although he didn't exactly hide well what he'd seen.

"Wait. You want to go in the bowling alley? You do know Michael is in there, right?"

"Michael who? Oh, him? I'm not asking you to take me to him. I just want some fries." The two walked off, both playing a role, leaving Bee to continue doing whatever it was she was doing.

Dear Hottywood,

I think my girlfriend is cheating on me. I'm not sure. How can I find out without falsely accusing her and jeopardizing my relationship?

Casper the Friendly Ghost

Dear Casper the Friendly Ghost,

Usually, I would suggest taking the direct approach, but seeing as how you're going on mere speculation, taking the direct approach will only lead you to a direct kick in the ass if your girlfriend is indeed being faithful to you. Things can get ugly if you're unsure and unprepared.

In most cases, if your gut tells you something is wrong, then you should listen. The gut never lies, unless of course you're lactose intolerant. If so, then your gut could be telling you that it's time to take a shit instead of sitting around waiting for shit to happen. Before you make any funky accusations you may want to take rest on a porcelain throne. In the meantime, here are a few tips that will help you to determine how much doo-doo has been dropped into the bucket.

If she has traded her sneakers and ratty old fairy dust slippers for stilettos, but isn't going anywhere with you to show off her sexy pumps, then the sweetness of your relationship could be turning into sour grapes. Also, pay attention to her hair and makeup, especially if she's a plain Jane, ponytail kind of gal who has suddenly pulled a Sandra Bullock ("Miss Congeniality") circa Y2K. If she's knocking boots with someone else, her appearance will matter a hell of a lot more with them than with you.

If she's not giving up any yum-yum and leaves you to fend for yourself in the bedroom, then you may want to trade in your baby oil for some dancing shoes in hopes of dancing your soon-to-be single ass into the arms of another.

If she seems to always hate you for nothing, chances are she's pissed with you for a reason . . . and that reason could most likely be because you are not the person that she would rather be with. If such is the case, save your breath, because as far as she is concerned anything you say at this point will suddenly become stupid and annoying.

Finally, watch out for the norms: excessive phone calls and text messages; date cancellations; increased use of perfume; and reminding you that you aren't owed any explanations for her actions.

If you see any of these signs, then that gassy feeling you have is your stomach's way of preparing you for the cliché that everyone hates to hear: "All good things must come to an end."

For your sake, I hope she's not cheating on you and that you're just paranoid. If, on the other hand, she has traded you in for an upgrade, then find comfort in knowing that I'll be right here if you need a shoulder to cry on, an ear to vent to, or a hanging partner when it's time to hit the singles bars!

"Aight, Boo. You good?" Bee's voice fell inside the black car upon the lap of an unidentified man donning a red bandana, to which she'd just finished giving special kisses.

"Am I good? Naw baby, you're the good one. Here."

A large hand passed a $50 bill outside of the window into Bee's hands. The car's engine revved loudly just before the tinted window scrolled up and the car drove off into the day. Bee watched as it sped out of sight, looking nonchalantly to see who, if anyone had witnessed her perverse act. Though she saw no immediate spectators, word of her whorishness had already begun to buzz about the center, reaching me before Willy. How the rumor got started and who started it is unknown. It wasn't as big of a deal as it would seem though. Giving blowjobs was not anything all too new for Bee. She wiped her bottom lip which felt moist and dry at the same time, afterwards applying a fresh coat of spaghetti and meatball flavored lipstick.

Inside the clamorous bowling alley walked Willy and Bird. I could almost hear Michael's heart hit the pit of his stomach as an invisible spotlight announced their entrance. At first glance I thought it was Bee hanging on Willy's arm until I quickly remembered the two never touched unless they were naked or at the bottom of a dark stairwell, so he could only be hobnobbing with the more ethical of the twins. Michael, on the other hand, needed no memory jog. His senses for Bird were like mine are for fried chicken. Awkward, I thought to myself. Feeling a sudden urge to pee and escape from a tense situation, I retreated to the bathroom. There's nothing more unattractive than standing among a group of people with a pee stain in your jeans. Not to mention I'd never live that down.

"Hey y'all, I'll be right back. I need to run to the little celebrity's room to put out a fire."

About five minutes later, Willy received a page. 4-1-1 is the number that flashed across the beeper's screen. Willy, studying the number curiously excused himself to retreat to the nearest payphone. Bird couldn't help but wonder if the call was from one of the girls he had been tipping with openly behind Bee's back. She didn't invest too much in the thought, though. She had more pressing matters on her mind. Moments after Willy walked off and seconds before Bird considered leap-frogging into the fry grease behind the counter after seeing Michael, Bee strolled in and rested her bum on the stool next to her sister.

"I think Willy saw you." Bird warned.

"So?" Bee wasn't fazed at the possibility of what Willy might have seen. Much like Willy, she didn't care what anyone thought of her. "If Willy saw me doing anything I shouldn't have been doing, it was because I wanted him to see. One thing you need to learn, Sis, is not to let anyone dictate your moves when they're walking the same way."

Bird knew exactly what, or to whom, rather, her sister was referring. She couldn't muster up a response because she felt morally strong that trading one bad deed for another was a sure way to get on the VIP list to hell. Every cliché Bee spat about Willy reminded Bird of the good she was missing with Michael. Watching him a few feet away didn't help matters any more. It almost made her want to go back on her word and retract her fishing hook of virtue. Bee's whorish words of wisdom continued.

"Look at him, Sis. He can't keep his concentration. He's missing you just as much as you're missing him. I'll tell you what you should do. Hike your skirt up a little bit and walk pass him. You don't have to say anything. Just look him in the eye and keep on walking. He's a man. He's going to think with the head in his pants and chase after you like a good little pet."

"Bee, the head in his pants is what got us into this mess in the first place."

"Sweetie," Bee replied, "when the head in a man's pants can't function, neither can the one on his shoulders."

"You know about head, don't you?" Willy, as he passed by, returned with reprisal in his voice.

"Hey Baby, there you are. I was looking all over for you." Bee attempted to hug Willy but he stopped her before she could wrap her arms around him. He rebutted sharply.

"Looking for me where, inside some nigga's lap?"

This was probably the exact moment that Bee realized words could impact just as greatly as any stick or stone. In the truest sense of a queen bitch, though, she retaliated in her usual boisterous way.

"What the fuck are you talking about? Don't talk to me like that." She jumped up in Willy's face, breaking just as bad as any dude getting ready to pop off, but Willy didn't budge. Steam came out of his nose. His light skin turned as red as a lobster.

"Bitch, sit down! I shouldn't even be talking to your nasty ass. Not with where your mouth has been. I know you were outside sucking my boy's dick."

"You don't know shit."

"I do know shit because I saw it for myself and it's just been confirmed." He waved his beeper in her face.

"Confirmed by who?"

"Don't worry about it. You aren't denying it so it must be true."

I'd retreated from the bathroom just as the argument heated up. The mood was tense. The air was thick and a large crowd was beginning to form.

"Aww . . ." Bee stood her ground. "You're mad because my mouth ain't been no further south than them bitches you've been fucking."

"I ought to punch you in your fucking mouth!"

"That would probably make you look like a bigger man than your little dick does."

And with her last quip, she found herself picking a tooth up off the floor. Everything happened so fast that everyone was too stunned to move immediately, except for Michael, who leaped over tall buildings in a single bound to protect his Bird-like Lois Lane from getting hurt on the humble. I dashed after him. I may not have known many things at such a young age, but I knew hitting a woman was something only punks do. Michael pushed Willy to the ground and for once stood taller than Willy's ego. Bird raced to help Bee clean the blood from her mouth, both sisters hiding behind the unmovable funny man who this time was seriously ready to kick butt.

"Get out of my way, Mike. I'm about to…"

"You ain't about to do nothing, Slim. Back down."

The boyish comedian had stepped into a grown man's shoes, protecting two women that both looked like the one he loved. Willy's roar simmered to a cat's meow. Just as security arrived, he scurried off with his tail between his legs.

Michael's rush to the twins' defense was all the apology he and Bird needed to reconcile their relationship. They didn't seal their reunion in words, but rather with a kiss. A big, wet, sloppy kiss that I was hoping I would never have to see in public again. Ever.

Regardless of how gross the PDA was, I was happy to see them together again. Michael was too cool of a guy and didn't deserve to be burdened with the depression of puppy-less love and Bird was too sweet. The story ended happily for everyone except Willy and Bee. Willy got knocked down by someone he thought he was bigger than and Bee finally got swatted for sucking the honey out of the wrong honey comb.

I never admitted aloud to anyone but my trip to the bathroom was a little more than that. Even though I knew Bee was a skank I still respected her more than I did Willy and I thought that she could do better than him. Although I didn't exactly have a well thought out plan, I figured if I told Willy what Bee had done that'd be a sure way to divide the two. They'd be broken up; Bird wouldn't have a reason to hang around Willy (since he'd no longer be dating her sister); and Willy would feel the pain of loneliness that Michael was experiencing, provided he cared about Bee half as much as his penis did. In my head that sounded like the simplest way to bust up our little group. Everyone may not have been happy per se, but again it wasn't a perfect plan. I didn't expect Bee to get a beat down – however, I have no control over karma. If you ask me, she should have had her ass beat for blowing some dude in public. Not only was that self-degrading and disrespectful to her man, it was just plain old dumb.

In the end, whether my plan was well thought out or not, everything worked out for the best. Michael came to his girlfriend's sister's defense, put his former best friend in his place and got the girl; Willy got his ego crushed; Bee learned the hard way that when you mess with fire your ass gets burned; and I never had to deal with Willy Shahoolahoop again. Stepping up my game to mind somebody else's business, with good intent in mind even though it caused Bee a tooth, was the least I could do for hating and encouraging Michael's separation from Bird for as long as I did.

My stepping in may have been unorthodox and slightly misplaced but it worked. Hottywood helped!

"Lying is a dish best served with a cold compress."

Two seasons passed and all talk of the Hype for Less drama seemed to be a thing of the past. Michael and Bird picked their relationship up where they left it before they went into the closet on the night of Willy's party. Bee continued to parade the streets holding close her crown as the baddest bitch in the Village. I'd begun to settle into my own confidence of rendering solutions to impossible problems. Willy withdrew himself from the crowd and soon began to roll with some busters from the northeast side of town. He was revered by some that witnessed his fist introduce itself to Bee's face, citing that she had it coming. Others deemed him a woman beater. One person was disappointed by the events of that day – Michael. He had finally seen Willy in the same dim light that Bird and I had seen.

  Their friendship wasn't the same after that. Willy's roll with a new crew didn't do anything to help salvage his relationship with us, his former crew, especially and specifically with Michael. In all the years that Michael had known Willy, he found out that he really didn't know him at all. Who was this supercilious tyrant that possessed the body of the cool kid he'd grown up with? Since the incident, the two only spoke in passing and it was awkward to see. It was funny to me but awkward nonetheless. Michael only looked at Willy with half eyes and

Willy's nerves trembled every time Michael opened his mouth. Bird refused to be anywhere near him and I didn't give a damn one way or another. Our friendship was based on a foundation of mere association. To me, Willy had always been disposable and in the end, I wanted to be the one to take out the trash.

☦

Early one Friday evening, all of the neighborhood regulars chilled on the twins' front stoop. There had to be at least twelve of us, including Michael and his brothers, Bird, and me. In usual jolly banter Michael entertained the crowd with his jokes. The street lights hadn't come on yet: Day was one yawn away from tucking itself in for the night. The sounds of our laughter dangled in the sky, no doubt stirring up the old hag across the street to call the police. There was a subtle breeze blowing in from the east and the air was crisp enough to send a shiver up a skeleton's spine. It was perhaps the brisk of the chill that allowed us all to see the fog sticking to the windows of the car that Bee had just gotten out of at the corner of the block. She looked at us in surprise, as if she wasn't expecting quite an audience. The car pulled off behind her, opting not to wait to see if she'd be okay walking through a rowdy gang. With pride, she continued with what her sister recognized as a walk of shame.

"Wuzzup, B? It's a little early for you to be coming in from a date, isn't it?" One of Michael's brothers greeted Bee as she joined us. He was perhaps one of the few remaining guys in the neighborhood, next to Michael and me, that hadn't sampled her sweet nectar. Bee didn't respond. Instead, she grabbed her sister's arm and dragged her in the house. No hello. No goodbye. Her rudeness fazed no one. Bee was boorish that way. It was a part of her charm.

Bird followed her inside with no surprise of the lack of unsubtly. The abrupt disruption validated Bee had done something ill-advised. She yanked her arm away from Bee and demanded some answers.

"What is wrong with you? What did you do?" For the first time in her life, Bee looked slightly disappointed in herself, though still half-heartedly cocky. She tried to avoid eye contact with Bird, but Bird was the only person who could see straight through her. "Bee, answer me. What's wrong?"

Bee sat her sister on a plastic slip covered couch in the living room. With a hesitant attempt to respond to the inquiry she replied by removing a large stack of bills from her purse. Bird's eyes widened.

"What's this? Where'd all this money come from?"

Bee finally mustered up a verbal response.

"You remember that guy I was seeing? The one from Hype for Less?" Bird shook her head concurrently. "He gave this to me."

"What do you mean he gave it to you? Why?"

Bee paused for a dramatic effect. "I, um . . . I told him I was pregnant . . . with his baby."

"You what?!" Bird was flabbergasted. She grabbed her sister's knee and peered closely into her eyes. "Are you?"

"Of course not."

"Well Bee, it wouldn't be the first time. You can't blame me for asking."

"I know, Sis. It's a little more complicated than that, though. See, the whole time I was messing with Willy, I was getting close to his boy to get even closer to the money everyone said his parents sent to Willy's grandmother. Willy was a goldmine, Girl. That's why I tracked him the way I did. Sherman, the dude from Hype for Less, was my cash-in ticket. He guarded Willy's house because of the money, which means he most likely knew where it was, so I started breaking him off on the side so I could have eyes on the inside. "

"Bee, please tell me you're lying."

"Does this look like I'm lying?" Bee referenced the stack of money. "Where else would I get all of this? I told you what happens when you mess with a man's head. When I told him I was pregnant, he freaked out just like I expected him to, and said he couldn't afford a baby any more than I could afford to take care of one. So I told him I'd get an abortion if he paid for it. I knew he couldn't afford it. That's when I suggested going in for the stash. He said he wouldn't do it, but I told him I'd tell Willy we were fucking the whole time behind his back if he didn't. I was banking on him being more afraid of Willy than of being a father. The next thing I knew, he scooped me up and gave me this. I didn't ask any questions, but I did get some new shoes. You like these?"

Bird was in awe as Bee modeled her new kicks. She didn't know what to say about her sister's latest scheme. Two halves of her sat on opposite sides of the fence of surprise. Both sides feared for Bee's life as well as her own considering they shared the same face. Mistaken identity was inevitable, she worried.

"So you're telling me you were messing with Willy all that time just for his money?"

"And the dick," Bee replied. "He looked like he could fuck."

"Could he?" Bird wondered.

"What do you care? You wouldn't know good dick if it…"

"If it what? Punched me in the face?"

Bird's sharp reply instituted a moment of silence briefly before gunshots echoed outside followed by the sound of voices scattering in terror. Bee dived to the floor while Bird dashed to the screen door to see what was going on, hoping everyone, especially Michael, was all right. Seconds later she saw a group of people running in the direction of Willy's house. Oh shit! She thought to herself. Without hesitation, she followed the crowd. Bee tailed.

The two arrived in front of Willy's only to see Sherman's car wrapped around a tree a few feet away from the house. Sherman's forehead lay buried on the steering wheel with two bullet holes in the side of the driver's door and a stack of bloody bills in the passenger's seat. Willy's grandmother stood in her front yard, wearing a floral moo-moo while holding a shotgun with both hands – smoke seeping from the barrel. Bee stood hidden behind a group of spectators, careful not to connect her dots to Sherman. Saddened from the pain of losing someone stupid enough to fall into her sister's even more stupid plan, Bird grabbed Bee and quickly fled the scene. Bee had once again succeeded in receiving something at someone else's expense, this time at an ultimate price.

☦

Looking back on those days, I can honestly say I understand why my mother tried to keep me in a bubble. Those blokes in the Village were some crazy motherfuckers. Sherman's death was the first time I'd seen anyone get killed, perhaps the first of too many. It put the term "love to death" in a whole new perspective.

Through it all I have no qualms about hanging with those characters, even Willy. He, along with Michael and the twins, introduced me to different stages of relationships. I watched a friendship and relationship grow and crumble. I witnessed, first-hand, how the rise and fall of both can have an effect on not only the persons involved but also the people around them. Willy proved to me that people can change and not necessarily for the better.

Michael and Bird taught me that honesty and communication is what is important in relationships and that love is not merely based on something physical.

Today, Michael and Bird are married and nursing two baby birds of their own. Twins – a boy and a girl. Their relationship has always reminded me of the behavior of actual birds, specifically the family of pigeons that shits on my windshield every morning. About ninety percent of birds are considered monogamous and oftentimes stay paired for the span of their lives. Conclusively, Michael and Bird showed me what I could expect out of love. Because of them, I am confident that no one has to conform to the norm of horny freaks and wannabes. No one has to spend cash or screw like a porn star to prove how much they care, which brings us to Willy and Bee.

Willy and Bee's relationship offered me the exact opposite of what I gained from Michael and Bird's. From them, I gathered sex does not constitute or justify emotion; what looks good to you isn't always good for you; and that kissing and telling discredits your credibility.

As far as I'm told, Bee, who is rumored to be unhappy and cursed with swollen ankles, still runs wild in the fast lane. She jumps from one relationship to another and has a closet full of flats to show for it. Given the sexual nature of bees, how ironic is it that Marlecka "Bee" Bagumgum follows suit of a real live queen honey bee?

Back in my school days, I can remember one time waking up before the end of science class just in time to catch the tail end of a rousing conversation about Apiology, the study of bees. In that lesson, my radar went up when I fell into a discussion about the mating of a queen bee and her drones (male bees). Who would have guessed that I'd be freaked out by a bunch of horny little insects?

I always thought that after bees mate, they die. Actually, only the drone dies. The queen lives on. Typically a queen bee will mate with anywhere between seven to ten (or more) drones. She has internal sacs that can store a volume of semen that would take at least eight drones to fill, so presumably any sexual encounters after those seven to ten drones is merely for pleasure. Whoever said all men are dogs obviously knew nothing about bees. Let me see if I can break this down into round-the-way terms.

First, let's be clear that a drone, AKA a male honey bee, exists entirely to mate with its queen. His sole purpose in life is to fuck and die. Is that a blessing or a curse?

Textbooks describe honey bee mating as the process where a drone inserts his genitals into the queen's reproductive tract. His ejaculation explodes like a volcano, with so much force that the tip of his genital ruptures, and is left behind in the queen. Once he's performed his royal duties he is of no further use to her and soon after plops to his death. I'm paraphrasing here.

Does this sound like a certain Bagumgum twin to you? Let's compare this sadistic sexual catastrophe with Bee's track record.

When a drone pulls away after mating with its queen (just before a dude pulls out of a woman, in this instance Miss Bee Bagumgum), its genitalia remain attached to her and are broken away (she uses her feminine wilds to strip him of his pride or his paycheck). The drone dies from its injuries (the dude's ego is crushed). The queen then removes the drone's genitalia and goes on to mate with another drone (Girlfriend gets what she wants out of the deal and moves on to the next man).

I believe the teacher that discussed this whole insect sex topic (way too enthusiastically) to my teenaged science class referred to the mating of honey bees as 'sexual suicide.' Raise your hand if you think this is an appropriate term.

Honey bee mating and the death of a drone are parallel to a trend of Bee's unsuccessful relationships. She's always been guilty of perpetuating sexual suicide just like the queen honey bee. She used guys for what she needed or wanted and then dropped them like hot potatoes. Because she was so busy not caring, she never considered how her reputation would both precede and succeed her. She may have gotten gifts after a good bang session – and good for her – but if you ask the wrong dude in the wrong neighborhood on the right day, he'll tell you trinkets are a small price to pay for ass. The reality is her relationships didn't fail because she was using what she had to get what she wanted. They failed because she told Victoria's secrets too much, too freely, or too soon.

☦

Thanks to the trails of my past, I'm diligent in advising people that relationships are as simple as the birds and bees. They'd be less complicated if people would relate their sexual behavior to the traditional story – be a Bird, born to love then make love or be a Bee, born to bone then die.

So now when I get questions pertaining to matters of the heart, I'm able to start my reply with my tape recorded response, *"Have I got a story for you."*

‡

Reverend Hottywood Presiding...

Reverend Hottywood:

Dearly Beloved, we are gathered here in Grandma Gertrude's kitchen in the sight of Jesus Christ AKA Heaven's very own DJ JC, and in the presence of all gathered witnesses, to join these two ninjas, Shereef Cupcake Starboots and Dequan Matthis Jenkins, Jr. III in Holy Matrimony, which is an honorable estate, instituted by DJ JC in the time of man's innocence (at least all the shit we don't know), signifying to us this mystical union of one reformed whore and pimp.

This union is not to be entered into lightly or inadvisably, but rather reverently, discreetly, and in the fear of the neighborhood police, Shaboinkin and the Loan Sharks, and God. Into which this Holy Estate Shereef and Dequan come now to be joined and to unite two hearts, two lives and two cookie jars filled with stolen liquor store money, blending all interest, sympathies, hopes, and brass knuckles. I charge and entreat you, therefore, in entering upon and sustaining this hallowed union, to seek the favor and blessing of He whose favor is life, whose blessing maketh rich and addeth no sorrow. Let us now seek His blessing.

Please bow your heads, but hold your purses and wallets tightly. We don't trust anyone in this neighborhood when our eyes are closed.

Dear Heavenly Father, we beseech Thee to come by Thy grace to this marriage. Give to these who marry a due sense of the obligations they are now to assume, so that with true intent, and with utter unreserve of love, or love of the baby that Ms. Shereef has growing inside of her since the pajama party at Lil Ray Ray's bachelor pad seven months ago, that they may plight their troth, and be henceforth helps meet for each other while they journey through life, as long as Dequan isn't punching Shereef in the mouth for not bringing home all of the hump money. This we ask in DJ JC's name. Amen.

Who gives this ho, Shereef Cupcake Starboots, in Holyish Matrimony to Pimp Daddy Dequan?

Father of the Bride:

I do, Your Highness. Darnell Starboots.

Reverend Hottywood:

I charge you both as you stand in the presence of the Father, the Son, the Holy Spirit, and the voice that only speaks to me when no one is looking, to remember that true love, loyalty, and the amount of cash you trade for sex with strangers, will avail as the foundation of a happy home. If the solemn vows you are about to make be kept inviolate, and if you steadfastly endeavor to do the will of your heavenly Father, your lives will be full of joy, and the home you are about to establish will abide in peace, so long as you not fall behind on your rent.

No other human ties are more tender, no other vows are more sacred than those you are about to assume, except those of Dequan's other two wives. You are entering into the Holy Estate which is the deepest mystery of experience, and which is the very sacrament of divine forced emotion from an unplanned pregnancy.

Dequan Matthis Jenkins, Jr. III, will you have Shereef Cupcake Starboots to be your awfully wedded wife, to live together on weekends after DJ JC's ordinance in the Holy Estate of Matrimony; will you love her, comfort her, not beat her regularly, honor, and keep her, in sickness and in health so long as you don't catch what she's got, and forsaking all others, keep yourself only unto her unless someone comes along with a price tag large enough to change your mind, so long as you both shall live?

Dequan Jenkins, Jr. III:

I guess so.

Reverend Hottywood:

Shereef Cupcake Starboots, will you have Dequan Matthis Jenkins, Jr. III to be your awful husband to live together on weekends after DJ JC's ordinance in the Holy Estate of Matrimony; will you submit to him, serve him, service him and all his pals, honor, and keep him, in sickness and in health and promise not to spread your legs or germs to any other man whose credit Dequan has not checked first, and forsaking all others, keep yourself only unto him, until he pimps you out and forces you to contradict these vows so long as you both shall live?

Shereef Starboots:

Fuck yeah!

Reverend Hottywood:

Dequan, what pledge do you give of the sincerity of your vows?

Dequan Jenkins, Jr. III:

The same ring I gave to my first and second wife. They're standing over by the refrigerator. Hey y'all!

Reverend Hottywood:

Shereef, do you accept this ring as a pledge of the sincerity of Dequan's vows?

Shereef Starboots:

I better or else he'll kick my ass. Sike. Yeah, I do.

Reverend Hottywood:

Dequan, repeat after me: With this ring, I Thee wed. And with all my worldly goods, including the candy I stole from your sister's baby last week, I Thee endow. In the name of the Father, the Son, the Holy Spirit, and the voice that speaks to Pastor Hottywood when no is around. AMEN.

Dequan Jenkins, Jr. III:

With this ring, I Thee wed. And with all my worldly goods, including the candy I stole from your sister's baby last week, I Thee endow. In the name of the Father, the Son, the Holy Spirit, and the voices that speaks to Pastor Hottywood when no is around. AMEN.

Reverend Hottywood:

And may this circlet of pure gold-plate which has no end, be henceforth the chaste and changeless symbol of your evermore impure and changeless affection, the same as it was to the other hoes you married and never divorced.

Shereef, what pledge do you give of the sincerity of your vows?

Shereef Starboots:

A Rolex watch that I ordered from the back of a comic book.

Reverend Hottywood:

Dequan, do you accept this fake ass watch as a pledge of the sincerity of Shereef's vows?

Dequan Jenkins, Jr. III:

I guess.

Reverend Hottywood:

Shereef, repeat after me: This watch I give you is a token and pledge of my sometimes constant faithfulness and cosign to half of everything that you earn and steal. AMEN.

Shereef Starboots:

This watch I give you is a token and pledge of my sometimes constant faithfulness and cosign to half of everything that you earn and steal. AMEN.

Reverend Hottywood:

May these symbols given be the outward and visible sign of an inward and spiritual bond which unites your two hearts in loveless lust that has no end. Forasmuch as Shereef and Dequan have consented in unholy wedlock, and have thereto confirmed the same by giving and receiving each one a fake ring and watch; by the power vested in me, I now declare you husband and wife. You may remove your gum and kiss the bride!

Ladies and Gentlemen, I present to you the President and First…ahem…Third lady of the project's ho stroll, Mr. and Mrs. Dequan Matthis Jenkins, Jr. III.

☦

Chapter 5

A Know-It-All's Nose Knows

Dear Hottywood,

What do you give to the person who knows it all and has everything?

Yogi

Dear Yogi,

This has to be one of the easiest questions to answer. Most people that think they have everything are missing one very important thing – humility. Since humility is something that can't be purchased, stolen, begged for, or even drawn, the best thing you can give someone who thinks they have everything is a big bag of nothing. After all, nothing is the cheapest gift you can get for someone who has it all.

When they brag about the material things that's been handed down to them, do not give them a comment to marinate on. When they tell an unfunny joke that they stole from a comedian on late night television, do not give them a chuckle. When they ask you for your advice which they probably think isn't worth anything, do not put in your $0.02. What's left to give? Say it with me class, "NOTHING!"

Giving the gift of nothing will probably do you a lot more good than the person you're giving the gift to. When they open that nicely wrapped gift only to find the contents of the box is missing, simply say, "Since you have everything, I figured nothing was the one thing you didn't have."

And like that empty box, they'll have nothing to say.

‡

Shortly after my britches bounced beyond the hill tops of the Village, my feet landed on unsettled soil. By the time I reached eighteen years old, I thought I'd seen enough turns of a new year to be able to say to myself with confidence that I wouldn't carry over any drama from one year to the next. Eighteen years was more than enough time to transition directly into adulthood, leaving behind my childhood comrades – Michael, Willy, Bird and Bee.

In my last hour as a seventeen year old, I knew it all. After all, I'd seen love at its best and worst. I'd broken people up and put them back together. I'd stolen cars, smoked weed, got arrested, and witnessed people die. What more to life was there? There wasn't much more of anything that anyone could show or tell me. It didn't take me long to graduate from the beginners class of the hills of Fairfax Village. I'd taken my first big step into a bigger world – a world full personalities drenched with more than just mushy emotions and hot pants; people that seemingly loved themselves and their opinions more than they did others; know-it-alls and wannabes; and that reminded me so much of myself – the good, the bad, and the stubborn. It was a new world that was my kind of town.

I remember one night hanging out in the wrong place at the wrong time with the wrong person.

It was a late Saturday night in the spring of '95. I was joyriding with a buddy of mine, Milwaukee Blue. Milwaukee was a true blood DC native, born and raised. He was cool. A funny guy, even though he talked a lot. He spoke in circles but never actually said anything. He always thought he was right, which by definition is a know-it-all, except of course when I do it, because I actually do know everything. He was a basic annoyance but entertaining nonetheless.

Milwaukee ran with an uptown crew and claimed to have marked his territory on the streets of DC like puppies pee on fire hydrants. He was a type cast black man. Unbeknownst to the casting society that he was indeed seeking to further his education, even though the degree he was seeking was a Bachelors degree from Clown College.

One day Milwaukee told me about a new carryout in town that he'd heard of called Pao Saki's Wings & Weaves. Not only did the wings taste like they came fresh out of a housewife's skillet, but girls went there to buy synthetic tresses, which also made the joint a great pick up spot.

Pao Saki's was up on 41st place, in the complete opposite direction of where we were at the time. Neither of us really knew how to get there, but my nose knew. Anyone that knows me knows that I'm the Sherlock Holmes of chicken wings. If there's a wing that's been dipped, fried and doused with salt, pepper and mumbo sauce, I can find it. Milwaukee, to no surprise, didn't believe in my GPS senses. Since he was "from the streets," he insisted on finding the joint with no help from me. His insistent denial of my confidence in direction was beginning to make me re-evaluate my tolerance for know-it-alls, present company, meaning myself, excluded.

We drove up and down every strip, street and stroll looking for Pao Saki's Wings & Weaves. For every right turn my nose told him to make, he made a left. Our joyride quickly took a dive. My taste buds were settled on hot wings while my stomach growled louder than the engine roared. Every one-way street and pothole we hit pissed me off more and more as Milwaukee continued to drive us into a deeper definition of lost.

I begged him to get out and lay in front of the car so I could drive back and forth over his fingers in an effort to take away his physical ability to drive, but nooooo. He thought that was a bad idea. Our quest for chicken wings had birthed a medieval joust between purpose and principle. His need to get us to Pao Saki's had become greater than my need for a bite of crispy deliciousness, briefly shedding light on him as being a selfish know-it-all (which is much worse than being a generic know-it-all). That only clashed with my self-proclamation of being Mr. Right and having a better idea of where the hell we were going. We were nothing more than two heads butting against each other turning out to look like asses in the end.

To make a long story short, as a result of him refusing to take heed to my instincts, Milwaukee finally drove us to a dead end street: Dead being the key word as a moderately sized army of hood rats with baby pythons wrapped around their necks surrounded our car. My fear of snakes was stronger than my fear of getting beat to death by guys that wore them as scarves. I must have scaled the walls like Spider Man or something because I got my ass out of there!

I remember running down the street clenching what was left of my bladder. Each sound of my footsteps hitting the pavement pounded out an S.O.S. to Jesus. About twelve blocks later, I finally looked behind me to see if I was being followed.

Thankfully the only things behind me were my pride and Milwaukee "Mr. Know-It-All" Blue. He was too embarrassed to say "You were right," and I was too mad to say "I told you so." We had come full circle to a dead end, minus the snakes.

I never did get any chicken that night. All I got was high blood pressure and achy feet. Milwaukee and I haven't spoken since, for obvious reasons. Those reasons heavily having to do with me not getting that chicken. Oh yeah, and almost being eaten by a nest of anacondas.

The memory of that night marks the first time I realized I couldn't put more trust in anyone than I do myself. I guess it's true what they say, "Those who think they know it all are really annoying to those of us that do."

Since then, as far as my world goes, there's only been room for one know-it-all – me! But my decree of knowing it all doesn't come unwarranted. I respond to what I'm asked. I help when solicited. I guide when someone steps onto my turf. I don't throw myself or my advice onto anyone, because I don't have the time, energy, or physical leg strength to be chased away.

I pride myself on holding all the answers to the universe on the basis of me not always being right while never being wrong.

"Everyone is different all the same."

Chapter 6
The Holy Hood Church of Mount Mattress Bedside Tabernacle

Staying true to my lineage of spirituality, I have to give credit to the church for introducing me to a whole new brand of people – heathens! Not only has church been the place where I attained an understanding of my faith, it harbored some of the most devilishly sanctified people. If that doesn't justify a single person's imperfections, I don't know what does. Because of such insight, I'm well equipped to spot all the warning signs of a person that lies like the devil.

☦

Somewhere on the corner between the firehouse and the gas station, around the block and three car washes away from home, sat a small little tabernacle where my grandmother raised her fourteen and a half children (my uncle is a "little person"). I'm sure it took the power of God to keep a single mother of that many kids from going all psycho every now and . . . always. In her house, there were three rules that the brood had to abide by: learn how to cook; submit to the fact that what Granny said went; and recognize the power in the name of Jesus.

Every Sunday morning, Granny dressed her kids in the finest tailored window curtains and carried them to Mount Mayhem, a small church in number though great in spirit. Mount Mayhem was my family's second home. Strong in participation from the choir to the flower club, Granny and the gang formed half of the congregation, which later grew into quite the mega church within three generations. The late Pastor Puss Bump, Mount Mayhem's co-founder and Granny's one time beau, left his son, Shugart Do Right Puss Bump, a reformed pimp, to rein dominion over the pulpit. Much like bullets out of the barrel of a gun, time shot small changes in the church that began with a drastic renaming calling out to the world by way of a flashing yellow sign that read, "OPEN ALL NIGHT". Mount Mayhem had now become The Holy Hood Church of Mount Mattress Bedside Tabernacle. And its members were just as entertaining as its name.

People from all walks of life came to celebrate the celebrity of the new Holy Hood. It was a church like none other. Service started whenever the pastor got there. Some Sunday morning worshippers spent the majority of their week at the church because the lower auditorium doubled as an after-hours speak easy. Every Tuesday through Thursday you were sure to find some deacon's offspring gambling away his tithes and offering in a game of Spades or Blackjack. But Sunday was the day when all souls could feel the heat of the lights, cameras, and action. It had gotten to a point where I, myself, had only gone to church for the show rather than the Word, which later came back to bite me in the ass. I wasn't the only one burned for messing with the Lord. In fact, the Holy Hood church was full of worshippers that misinterpreted the Bible and the warnings of judgment day.

I can remember one particular Sunday morning like it was yesterday. It began like any other. Children on the back pew passing notes; Elder Eunice "Granny Cakes" Wilya Poo-Poo's super big, polka dotted hat rocking from side to side; the ushers on either side of the church dozing off in their folding chairs.

Pastor Shurgart Puss Bump sat on a 14k gold plated throne-like chair, high on the pulpit. Behind him in the choir stand sat LaQuisha ShaQuan Odell Muhfukin Palmer, her sidekick, LaToya Evans, and the 6" High Heel Chorus.

Sister Gabby Gossip, the church clerk, with her fishnet stockings and 5" stilettos, was the only woman that sat on the front pew with the deacons. Among them were Deacon Pimp Gigolo, Deacon Day-Day, and the backup singers for the Get Back Crew, who were also the ministers of music. There also sat Chum Murphy, the church percussionist. He, by no fault of his own, was rhythmically inept.

Some say he couldn't focus on his timing because he was too busy chasing after LaQuisha and LaToya. Others say he was jittery from all the weed he smoked.

I, like the rest of the guys in the church anxiously awaiting the afternoon football game, skimmed through the bulletin to estimate a time for the end of service, just as Sister Gabby prepared to stand before the congregation to render the weekly announcements.

Holy Hood Church of

Mount Mattress Bedside Tabernacle

Sunday Worship Guide

Sunday, November 12, 2000

10:52am

El Libro Sagrado de los Tacos

Page 129, 1st Verse: Satan gave me a taco.

Call to Worship, Invocation…………................

    Pastor Shugart Do Right Puss Bump

Processional…………………………………….

    Give It To Me Right Senior Choir & the 6"

    High Heel Chorus

Selection……………………………………...

    Give It To Me Right Senior Choir

Scripture Reading……………………………….

    Heratio Fellatio Jenkins, Jr.

    Book of Bottle Caps 3:14-18 ~ Praying Out of
    a Brown Paper Bag

Prayer..
    Sister Nita Mindyo Bidness

Welcome...
    Elder Eunice "Granny Cakes" Wilya Poo-Poo

Church Announcements.............................
    Sister Gabby Gossip, Church Clerk

Selections...
    6" High Heel Chorus featuring The Heaven's

    Gates Pitbull Band

Tithes and Offering....................................
    Deacon Day-Day and the Get Back Crew

Offertory Prayer/Response..........................
    Deacon Pimp Gigolo

Meditational Solo......................................
    LaQuisha ShaQuan Odell Muhfukin Palmer

    "There's a Place in Hell Even for Me"

Gospel Message..
    Pastor Shugart Do Right Puss Bump

2nd Offering for the Feed the First Family So They Never Have to Spend Their Own Money in the Grocery Store Fund..

    Pastor's Aide Ministry,

    Brother P.W. BeatUDown, President

Call to Discipleship......................................

    Pastor Shugart Do Right Puss Bump and the Ministers' Mistresses of Mount Mattress Bedside Tabernacle

Exit Fee Offering...

    Brother Homer Yuckmouth and Trustee Newton Noknow

Benediction...
Pastor Shugart Do Right Puss Bump

*Chicken wings, french fries and jumbo iced-tea served in the lower auditorium for a small free will offering fee of $19.95 (plus tax).

"Good Mawning, Church," Sister Gabby rallied the church, her voice high and loud with a cute southern twang. "I said, 'Good Mawning, Church!'" she repeated. "This is the day that the Lawd has made. I know there ought to be somebody in here that knows this is a good mawning. Now can I get a 'Good Mawning?!'" Her voice elevated with a reverent liveliness that stirred the congregated souls. The church, almost in synchronized time, responded with a chorus of hallelujahs.

"That's what I'm talking 'bout," she continued. "I thank Him! I thank my Jesus for allowing me to see another day. He didn't have to do it, but He did. And if that ain't good, I don't know what is!" The crowd encouraged her testimony.

"I don't know about you but I came to praise the Lawd! Yessuh!" Her inner evangelist inched its way out of her leather bustier. "And I'm gon' praise Him even if I have to praise Him all by myself! Heeeey!"

She jumped up and down, along with her boobs, as the Get Back Crew grabbed their instruments and cranked up a boisterous tune of the church's theme song, "Ain't Got No Bootleg God." Hats flew, ladies in JFJ (Jamming for Jesus) miniskirts danced in the middle of the aisles while brothers inconspicuously placed bets on the colors of their underwear.

Sister Gabby, in her usual diva-like way, settled the people. "Y'all bet' not get me started up in here! Ain't that right, Pastor?"

"That's right, Sista," slurred the Pastor. "That's all right, Baby." Heavy on the "all."

Gabby regained her focus, wiping sweat from her bosom with a laced handkerchief. "Let us turn our attention to the bulletin for the morning announcements. Pastor, if I may, following the announcements I'd like to ask Brother Badcheck to lead us in a word of prayer before the selection from the 6" High Heel Chorus . . . because Lawd knows we're going to need some prayer to get through that."

Tucking her boobs inside her bustier, she continued with the program.

"First we have a special note from Mother Mays . . ."

CHURCH ANNOUNCEMENTS

Special Notice: Free Will Offering

There will be a $5.00 minimum cover charge for all meals served under the Free Will Offering program to get new spinners for Mother Mays' turbo wheelchair. All meals will still be served at the corner of 5th and Stank Avenue, between the laundromat and Herb's Carwash.

-Mother Bertha Mymanzaho Mays, MMBT Meals on Wheels, Chairperson

---

Mass Choir Rehearsal

Thursday, November 16, 2000 – 6:01pm

All choirs are asked to meet at Roscoe's Poles and Holes next Thursday instead of the church sanctuary. The church is being evaluated for disco ball installation and must be vacant during the consultation process. Members are asked to brush their teeth before showing up for rehearsal because Roscoe's is kind of small.

-Briefcase Daddy O., Jr., Emeritus Minister of Music

Ice Cream Social

Friday, November 17, 2000 – 6:42pm

The Hoodlums-in-Training Youth Department will hold an ice cream social for all persons who are not as big as cows and are not lactose intolerant. Be advised that those who violate the stipulations of the invite will burn in hell.

-MMBT Youth Department

Special Prayer Request

Please remember, in prayer, all persons who get caught with stolen credit cards while using them to illegally sell gasoline to customers at gas stations in return for dollars to later hit up the liquor store for false communion wine. There has been a string of occurrences near the pump station over by Roscoe's Poles and Holes.

Bout Damn Time Health Ministry

The ministry of fat asses will meet next Tuesday at 7pm. Please enter through the double doors at the side street entrance.

Usually, a church that prays together stays together

Pastor Shugart peered over his dark shades to take in the sight of Sister Gabby's long, fish-netted legs as she rendered the announcements, surreptitiously covering his unchristian like fantasies of pouring fried shrimp and ketchup all over her body.

Roberta Mean Face sat on the pew adjacent to the deacons with the rest of the deacons' wives, each of them wearing long, white skirts and holding Bibles in their laps. Roberta watched Gabby's every move like a hawk. She and the rest of the deaconesses never smiled, but were still nice ladies, except when Gabby got up. To them, Gabby was the devil, though they were unsure whether or not she was sleeping with the pastor.

Not only was she tantalizing eye candy and wore a mean hat cocked to the side, Sister Gabby was a big personality and carried weight in the church. She was charismatic enough to captivate any audience and was known for her impeccable timing, whether emceeing a formal function or dominating an informal conversation. As the official clerk, she kept the church's books, monitored the pastor's emails, and supported all of his pastoral needs, the needs of the church and a select group of its members. She was like the crypt keeper of an unlocked vault to everybody's business, and within this position laid her biggest problem: she couldn't keep running water. This free-spirited, wise-cracking, fishnet-wearing gate keeper was the person everyone wanted to be around, but never wanted to get close to. She was as dangerous as her high heels looked. Gabby loved a good piece of gossip and she loved to tell it. Gossip to her was like Crack. Get close to her, if you dared. She would throw your ass under the bus quicker than you can say, "Oh no she didn't!" No one ever made mention of her loose lips aloud because she always had the best underground bulletin talk. She was also unafraid to put you in your place if you got her wrong. She was one venomous bitch that didn't mind a good cat fight. Still, while Gabby may have been a nosey heifer, there was something to gain from her; and that was the business of making it a business to know other people's business. It's always important to know what other people are doing to stay ahead of the pack, especially when that pack is on your ass for knowing too much.

"This concludes our morning announcements. And as we like to say here at the Holy Hood Church of Mount Mattress Bedside Tabernacle, 'Usually, a church that prays together stays together.'"

Sister Gabby gathered her notes and sashayed back to her seat. Taking her place at the podium was Brother Morty Badcheck, a part-time trustee young in spirit and old in dog years. Morty wore a throwback, velour Fila track suit, complete with an oversized gold-plated rope chain, fuzzy Kangol fedora, and Hebrew sandals paired with white socks. He was a prayer warrior that spent many long hours on the pay phone up the street from the church praying for his lost brothers and sisters in Christ. His prayers were usually longer than the wait for the delivery of a Dominos pizza, but definitely worth the listen. He was one of those wannabe young old-heads that waited an entire lifetime to grow old enough to say whatever he damn well pleased. And so he did.

"My black people, my blue-eyed soul brothers and sisters, and all y'all folk that wear too much makeup to pinpoint what nationality you are, let us bow our heads in a word of prayer."

Members across the sanctuary snickered at the candidness of Brother Badcheck's prayer opening.

"Gracious God our Father, I come to you Lord first to say, 'Thank you.' I thank you for my lying down last night and waking up this morning. I thank you for the sweet potatoes and corn pudding that Sister

Yvette brought over to my house last night. And Father, most of all I thank you for making that fine young lady's pregnancy test negative. You alone know I'm too old to be a father to another baby's baby. You know I can't afford to pay another dime out of my social security check. The only things I can afford these days are a pack of cheese and fifteen minutes at the Chinese massage parlor. But only you, Father God…only you can see me through."

The congregation moaned like slaves, praying on one accord.

"Bless him, Lord!" A voice from the congregation cried out.

"Now, Lord," Badcheck continued, "there are some souls in here that needs healing, beginning with the little bastard that stole the money out of the Young Strippers Ministry's petty cash box. Nobody knows whose hands were vile enough to take that money, but You, Oh Father. But I know if I'd have seen it for myself, God, that you would have given me the strength to whoop that ass something good. You would have given me a renewed strength to karate-chop that thief all up and down the aisles of this church. Glo-ry!"

Once again, the church erupted in an uproar. Little Johnny McMillerhoff slid deep in his seat of the pew, looking to see who (if anyone) was watching him, beads of sweat streaming down his face. The echo of Brother Badcheck's words poked him. It was clear Johnny had a few sins that begged repentance, but those secrets were supposed to be between him, God, and a midget whose name he vowed to keep to himself for fear of getting jumped by a band of little people in the parking lot (I assume, bearing no association with my uncle). At that very moment, Johnny felt an unsettling presence embrace him as his name was being written on the guest list to Satan's weekend bash.

"Lord, forgive me!" Johnny shouted from his seat, hands tossed to the air. "The devil made me do it! Forgive me, Father! Forgive me!" With a heavy heart, Johnny cried like fresh meat in a state penitentiary. Embarrassment wrote itself across his forehead. The heat of the spotlight was soon cooled by Mrs. P. Gertrude, RN, a registered nurse and a Mary Kay makeup sales associate, who hustled the product more than hustlers push dope, as she rubbed Johnny's back in a motherly manner. The aroma of her cannabis breath calmed his upset while enticing his need for something sweet to eat. Sister Gabby once told me that nurse Getrude is the person Chum

Murphy got his weed from. She said, "Petunia got that fire!"

‡

Dear Hottywood,

I've been a member of a small church for a number of years. Recently, one of my deepest, darkest secrets was exposed and circulated among the congregation. I am so humiliated that I'm considering changing my membership. Would you recommend I do that?

Skeletons Out of the Closet

Dear Skeletons Out of Closet,

Hell no, you shouldn't change your membership! There are two groups of people on the face of the planet that can ruffle a tail feather more than any other group: family members and church members. If you've been a member of your church for a number of years, then you should know, first-hand, that the church house is full of holy heathens and well-dressed short comers.

You don't go to church for the sake of anyone else (unless of course you've just been released from prison and are forced to live in your grandmother's basement with the sole stipulation that you take your criminal butt to church to thank Jesus for letting you out of your cellblock before your fully tatted boyfriend finally got tired of your fresh meat and passed you around to all the other inmates inside and outside of that block). And though you go to fellowship with those of like-minded spirits, the first reason that you should be going to church is to commune with the Main Man himself. The next is to confess your sins and lay your burdens down. The last thing you should be concerned about is fraudulent, sanctified soul stirrers that are more concerned with stirring up trouble than they are with saving their butts from burning in an eternal pit of fire.

Every church, including yours, no doubt, has a Sister Church Gossip, a Deacon Ned Wino, a Mother Midnight Creep, a Brother DL, a reformed pimp, prostitute, thief, ex-con, woman beater, and/or a habitual liar. I say this to remind you that you are not the only one that has fallen short of His Word. In fact, all are born into sin and no one sin is any greater than another, well…with the exception of skinless, fried chicken wings. There is no salvation for that!

Since you are too clean in heart to curse your hypocritical holy rollers like the devil, to ease your troubled mind, refer to your Bible beginning with Malachi 4:1-3.

It states: "1The LORD Almighty says, 'The day of judgment is coming, burning like a furnace. The arrogant and the wicked will be burned up like straw on that day. They will be consumed like a tree – roots and all. 2But for you who fear my name, the Sun of Righteousness will rise with healing in his wings. And you will go free, leaping with joy like calves let out to pasture. 3On the day when I act, you will tread upon the wicked as if they were dust under your feet,' says the LORD Almighty."

Those members that seem so amused by your tainted past will have a price to pay come judgment day. And while you are standing on the other side of the pearly gates upon streets paved with gold, they will be preparing to bungee jump into the devil's lair with no ropes, no nets, and no water to quench their thirst after their un-stealthy arrival in Tartarus.

‡

One by one, emulating jumping beans, the members of MMBT bounced from their seats with their hands raised higher than their hair weaves and high top fades. LaQuisha ShaQuan Odell Muhfukin Palmer was the next to stand in prayer. She could scoop soot from a fireplace with her long, acrylic, fluorescent press-on nails. She hung her head low and leaned forward slightly, exposing a brand new boob job doused with an excessive amount of baby powder. Her prayer was solemn.

"I just want to thank you, Lord, for making me a blessing to my home girl, LaToya. All her life, she's been a chicken head that ain't never had no real friends, until you sent me to her to make her look more popular than she is. You know she can't help that she ain't got nothing. It's not her fault that every time we go to the club, I have to dance an extra lap around the pole to be able to afford to pay for the both of us. I thank you for making me that kind of a friend, Lord. A real ride or die bitch. God, you didn't make LaToya stank for no reason. You made her stank so she could appreciate the life she could live if she ever one day finds her way to a truck stop. I ask that you shower blessings upon the blisters on her feet that bulge out the side of her cheap shoes. I told her to stop wearing those cheap shoes, but she won't listen to me, Lord, so I pray that she listens to You or somebody under the sound of your voice. She doesn't really listen to anybody, though. That's why she doesn't have anything. But she has me, Lord. And she has You."

LaToya's zit infested dark skin turned maroon as LaQuisha prayed. Sister Gabby's eyes were wide with disbelief and the deaconesses had finally broken their botox frowns. Nurse Getrude had calmed Jimmy enough to rest comfortably back in her seat while continuing to stuff weed into dime bags under her bulletin. Pastor Shugart remained in his seat, looking as cool as any 1970s pimp with a built-in gangster lean.

"Praise Him, Sister!" Praise Him!" Sister Gabby called from the front pew. "Praise Him louder so I can hear you …"

With every word that vomited from LaQuisha's mouth, tears welled in LaToya's eyes. Stunned by the hurtful reveal of her best friend, animosity filled her. At a particular moment, I could almost hear her heart and brain simultaneously stop on a second of spite. A marquee of Deuteronomy 3:22 flashed across the windows of her eyes. Somebody's scroll was about to be unfolded.

☦

"Egotism is nature's asprin for stupidity."

Just before armpit stains settled and roller curls fell, the 6" High Heel Chorus, finally following the order of the program, rendered a moving selection of the church's classic hymn "Coming Clean on Judgment Day." The group of six voluptuous bombshells, all in perfect step with the Get Back Crew's funky bass line, graced the congregation with a beautifully choreographed, liturgical rendition of the electric slide. Everybody in the room swayed to the beat, all but getting up to join in on the popular line dance.

LaQuisha, the lead singer and showboat of the group, did her regularly scheduled somersault in the center aisle, carrying a cordless microphone in her garter belt. She landed on a high pitched trill only a dog could hear. No one could hold back any tears, mainly because their heads were about to explode. The window cases rattled slightly, scaring members in the immediate line of fire of a possible glass shatter. At first the crowd fell to the ground, like anyone would if they heard gunshots at close range. But when they realized the note was a part of the act, they all stood to their feet and cheered.

Angered by the applause, LaToya from out of nowhere spun from the front of the back line and stole the note right out of LaQuisha's mouth. It was the first time she had ever stepped outside of

LaQuisha's shadow. She had the voice of an angel. Who would have guessed that a girl with three kids and four possible baby daddies could sing like that? Suddenly all of the colors in the sanctuary transitioned to a virtuous white, matching the color of the group's patent leather cat suits. A heavy layer of calm hovered over the room. Jaws dropped. Silence fell. Peace. Be still.

In the midst of all the theatrical commotion, a quivering voice sailed over my head from three pews behind my usual seat, where I sat with Granny and the rest of the family. Brother Paul Will Beatudown, the president of the Pastor's Aide ministry, stood to offer a word of testimony.

Brother Paul was a big man. Often dressed in some sort of silk paisley printed shirt unbuttoned to his navel, he spoke very little. Many feared him because of his size. He was almost big enough to occupy an entire pew by himself, no doubt from all the cheeseburgers that he had stashed away in the glove compartment of his car. No one ever dared to advise him to go on a diet. He was easily offended and had no problem punching anyone in the lip for crossing a line of disrespect. I, on the other hand, was more afraid of him sitting on me than I was for him to punch me in the face. I never ruled out him eating me either, especially since many of the church ladies told me that I was the sweetest thing they'd ever seen.

"Brother Pastor, if I may. The Lord sees fit to move me to speak from the heart."

Taken aback from Brother Paul's public request, Pastor Shugart nodded in concurrence. "Go right on, my brother. Ain't nobody mad but the devil."

"It is no secret that I've beat up many men on the grounds of this kingdom. For that I do not apologize because most of them had it coming." Many of the men to whom Brother Paul referred turned their heads away in an effort not to remind him of why he beat them up in the first place.

Paul continued. "I am not proud of my actions but I am proud to say that those people will not cross me again. My burden, Church, rests in my inability to sustain any more tolerance for my family. My children are disobedient. My wife, one of the lovely members of the 6" High Heel Chorus, is harboring a secret that is tearing up our happy home. My mother is on probation for stealing hubcaps off a Toyota Camry for her senior limited-edition rollerblades and I am at my wits end. I only know how to resolve my problems with violence . . . and cheeseburgers.

Personally, I vowed never to step foot inside another jail cell, not because there are no windows, but because they don't offer seconds on the meals. Romans 13:4 tells us, 'For he is God's servant for your good. But if you do wrong, be afraid, for he does not bear the sword in vain. For he is the servant of God, an avenger who carries out God's wrath on the wrongdoer.' I quote this scripture almost every day as I deal with the issues of my broken home. I stand before the church this day to ask for a special prayer that I don't start handing out whippings inside my house. My parole officer, an angel sent from heaven or someplace like it, told me never to whoop another ass if I want to stay out of jail . . . assuming he doesn't know I'm aware he's sleeping with my wife, hence the secret she is keeping from me. Somebody please pray for me. Pray for my strength. Pray for my family." He bowed and shook his head with a somber conviction.

The floor of the church had become wet with drool. Brother Paul's testimony moved everyone in the building in one way or another. His wife's eyes bulged before her tears flowed, mostly because she knew he was going to leave her ass after church or kick it when she got home. His children froze in their seats, their fingers crippled from passing notes of jest to their friends. The brothers in the congregation found a moment of relief, reveling in the verity that his resentment had fallen upon his own tribe.

Brother Paul let out a vociferous whimper, enough to shake the Bob Marley pictures hanging on the walls. Even Gabby felt a sort of remorse for him, though not enough to avoid recording half of his juicy testimony inside her bulletin. Overcome with emotion, he fell to his seat with his face buried in the palms of his hands and like a real man, cried like a bitch.

Dear Hottywood,

Not too long ago I got myself wrapped up in a financial bind. I turned to family for help – I'm still determining if that was a good idea or not. Since turning to them, all of my business has been circulating amongst the family circuit. I'm tempted to withdraw my request for help, although I still need it. What should I do?

Strapped for Cash

Dear Strapped for Cash,

Everyone needs help. I know how stressful it can be to need help and have to deal with petty bullshit on top of the stress you're already dealing with. But let's face facts – and these are your words, not mine – "I'm tempted to withdraw my request for help, although I still need it." You need to swallow a big chunk of humble pie and get over yourself long enough to steer clear of this bind you're tangled up in. Why do I say that?

If all your business is circulating among your family, you've nothing to hide. The damage is done. If your family is helping you get your priorities straight, it shouldn't matter who's telling your business. That's most likely the least of your concerns. If they're helping you, especially financially, they've paid for their right to discuss your affairs. At least that's the way they see it. You should be more worried about getting yourself out of your bind than protecting your ego. Own up to the mistake you've made then learn from it so you don't be the same fool twice. Being adamant about your privacy is going to make you look crazier than the mess you've gotten yourself into because you're putting your focus in the wrong place.

Family is going to talk about you. That's what they do. If they are discussing your business behind your back, who cares? They've probably been discussing you before all this mess got started and will continue to do so when it's all said and done. You're still getting the help you need right? Suck it up and take the bitter with the sweet. They're getting the satisfaction of having some juicy gossip while you're getting the satisfaction of having someone do for you that which you can't do for yourself. It may feel unfair, but it's an even trade.

Rest in the comfort of knowing that everyone screws up from time to time; and for every good and bad thing that you do, someone has or will do something better or worse. Take a chill pill and relax. Before you know it, you'll be the one talking about someone behind their back. Then the world can revolve around you and everything will be back to normal.

☦

Brother Badcheck, annoyed, tapped his fingers upon the top of the podium, watching all of the members steal the shine from his prayer. With no intended fault of the congregation, they had completely forgotten that he was standing before them, performing like a slapstick church scene straight out of a D-list movie. Out of nowhere, a loud hiss echoed from the microphone speakers, interrupting the disorder. Everyone was startled, but not quite surprised, to see Brother Badcheck chugging a grape soda.

Finally fed up with the disrespect of his aide, Pastor Shugart put down his communion wine goblet and strutted to the pulpit. Choosing his words carefully, he rendered a personal address to Brother Badcheck.

"Excuse me, Cat Daddy, but you do know this is a church, right? Drinking anything other than the fruit of the vine is not acceptable in the sanctuary."

I thought to myself, 'Seriously? All that is going on and the only thing you are worried about is a pop?'

"But Pastor," Brother Badcheck replied, "you can't get anymore fruitier than this vine here. It's grape soda – the other communion wine. Whatever. I guess since the church has finished the prayer that I started, all that's left for me to do is hope that Brother Hottywood answers my prayer and drops me off up the block when service is over. As long as I've been standing up here while you all have been carrying on, my dogs are killing me!"

Surprised didn't quite describe the way I felt at that moment. There was only one question that kept running through my mind: How can I tell an almost faithful Christian (almost meaning he almost goes to church every Sunday) of God to go to hell? Granny looked at me closely, monitoring the expression on my face. Mama Hottywood turned away, pretending as if she didn't know me for fear of what my response might be. Thankfully, I was raised with enough sense to believe, or at least pretend to, that the Holy Hood Church of Mount Mattress Beside Tabernacle was a place of worship and respect, even for heathens. I was also afraid that Granny would slap the taste out of my mouth if my answer looked like it was going to begin with the letter N and end with an O. Pissed off by the obligation to say "yes," I nodded in agreement, secretly calculating the fare I was going to charge Brother Badcheck for putting his white socks and sandals in the back seat of my car.

Thou Shalt

Kiss my

Butt!

Amen.

The rest of the service continued as normally as one would expect for any church that operates terribly outside of the norm. Pastor Shugart delivered a moving sermon about raspberry iced tea being God's favorite flavor, followed by a praise break dance contest between the Golden Agers and the Junior Jam for Jesus Cheerleaders. After the spiritual pep rally, the deacons and ushers came forward to set up for the third and final offering. You could almost hear the reverberation in the members' pockets as they scrounged for loose change. Small coins, as long as they were silver, didn't matter to the trustees. In their eyes, it all added up to enough dollars to keep the pastor driving around town in a pimped out dune buggy. The members stood to their feet, waiting to be led by the ushers to the portable ATM machines when out of nowhere things took a sudden turn.

Grady Burns, a longtime member of MMBT and known wino, made his way to the front of the sanctuary. His clothes were dingy and wreaked of Noxzema skin cleanser and TOP paper. Though he remained questionable in his outward appearance, he was a very gifted speaker, even if underestimated upon first glance and whiff of alcohol and outdoors. It was amazing to hear fifty point Scrabble words cross the same lips that caressed the can of a malt liquor beer.

As he approached the podium, he looked carefully into the eyes of certain church members. His gaze was frightfully hypnotizing. No one knew his purpose for interrupting the service and going off script. All eyes were on him. Even Pastor Shugart sat with glazed eyes.

"My dear people of the church," Grady said, clearing his throat for a smooth delivery. "After taking witness to the spirit of this service, my soul feels compelled to speak to the masses of sinners that breathe the devil's wrath under the guise of the worship of the Master. I am utterly disappointed in the way you have carried on in this house today. Ashamed at the side eyes, the undertones, and the prayerful backstabs. You said-Christians are no better than the bums that contend with me for spare change in front of the liquor hut. A purely righteous man would have walked out of here long ago with his head hung low from the mockery of your adulation. However I, according to many of you, am not a righteous man. According to you, I am just a bum who is well versed in bottom shelf liquors. I stand not before you to pass judgment on your playhouse praise, but rather to speak on behalf of the lost souls that come to church for a word from a shepherd that leads his sheep away from wolves instead of towards them."

No one uttered a word in response to Grady's witness. No one snickered. No one budged. A silent gloom fell over the chancel. Even Brother Paul's big ass felt small. Gabby's pen ceased to sail across the free space of her bulletin and the pastor all but got up and walked off the pulpit.

"I may not rise to the standards of your ideas of a Christian but I am by far closer to the gates of heaven than any of you. You all ought to be ashamed to damn those whose sins you deem greater than your own. I wish to thank you for helping me and those of my kind to see that the face of the unrighteous rests even behind coveted walls. My indulgence shall one day cease to arouse me because I am sure that God is not through with me yet. Greater things are in store as I endure my troubled nights and anxiously await the joy that is to come in the morning. By damning me, each other, and mocking the name of all that is holy, you have all damned yourselves to an eternal pit of raging fire where water will do you no good. The bible says, 'For he that eateth and drinketh unworthily, eateth and drinketh damnation to himself, not discerning the Lord's body. For this cause many are weak and sickly among you, and many sleep.' I think I can speak for my fellow transgressors when I say, 'May all who gloat over my distress be put to shame and confusion; may all who exalt themselves over be clothed with the same shame and disgrace.'"

At the very moment when the church would usually blend their voices to recite the ever popular "Amen!," no one spoke a word except for the one man in the back of the church who brought his own communion wine. He stood proudly with his bottle raised in the air and said, "I'll drink to that."

☦

It should come as no surprise that I no longer attend the Holy Hood Church of Mount Mattress Bedside Tabernacle. Not because I lost interest. Not even because I questioned the intent of its members, but rather because not long after Grady's monologue the church closed down due to an intense government tax fraud investigation. The tabernacle's members got caught with green dye on their red hands.

From my understanding, today Pastor Shugart is in jail on four counts of fraud to the third degree. It took six years for Sister Gabby Gossip to wake up from a coma after finally being jumped by the deaconess board. There are now only three living members of the 6" High Heel Chorus. They can be seen every Tuesday, Thursday, and Saturday night at Clancy's Topless Pizzeria over on Good Hope Road. The pizza's not that great, but no one goes there for the food.

Lastly, Brother Morty Badcheck finally came into some money when he opened a covert chicken trafficking operation in the woods behind the outhouse in the back parking lot of the former Holy Hood Church . . . MMBT. The operation didn't last very long, for obvious reasons, but for the time that business was booming it was a major success, particularly among the Chinese carryout owners in the area. He is now married to Ming Lee Wongfongo, the owner of Ming Lee's Chinese Chicken-Flavored Yak Burgers. They are happily expecting their third child, and he is able to meet the alimony payments on all of his other illegitimate children.

I don't know if it's fair to say things turned out well for all the members of the Holy Hood Church of Mount Mattress Bedside Tabernacle. Things did however turn out the way they were intended according to the Lord's plan. From that era of my past, I augmented the truth that when you play with God all hell breaks loose.

I still attend church every week with my family. A real church. One with the word 'Baptist' in the title. That's not to say there are no sinners there. To say that would be a sin in itself. Thanks to Granny and her root in religion, as well as to the sinners of the Holy Hood Church of Mount Mattress Bedside Tabernacle, I can attest that no one is perfect, not even the man that profits from the gain of the world at the expense of his soul.

Ending on that note, let the people of the church say, "Amen."

Are You a Tithing Member of
The Holy Hood Church of
Mount Mattress Bedside Tabernacle?

Rate Yourself.

It doesn't take much to become a member of the Holy Hood Church of Mount Mattress Bedside Tabernacle. With a little laziness, scandal, and some effort in being trifling, you too can have courtside seats at the devil's arena. Just be sure to pack a water bottle because things tend to get a little hot!

1. You've shown up for church hung over from the night before. **20 points**
2. You've brought your own communion wine to church. **60 points**
3. You've hooked up with another church member during service. **60 points**
   a. If that church member was the pastor, a deacon or deaconess, **add 40 points.**
4. You use curse words in your prayers. **10 points**
5. You are a choir director, but cannot sing and only listen to hardcore rap. **10 points**
6. Your church bylaws come from a Hollywood gossip magazine. **40 points**
7. You've re-enacted the Lord's Supper or the Last Supper at a McDonald's food chain. **30 points**

8. You've shown up for church without wearing any underwear. **10 points**
9. You've shown up for church wearing someone else's underwear. **20 points**

Holy Hood Church of Mount Mattress Bedside Tabernacle Membership Rating

0 – 60 You are almost but not quite a serious sinner.

61 – 100 You either need Jesus or a psychiatrist.

101 – 160 You need to be hosed down with holy water.

161 – 300 Pack your bags. You are on a permanent vacation to hell!

After the shenanigans of the Holy Hood Church of Mount Mattress Bedside Tabernacle, it dawned on me that I hadn't learned everything there was to know about the world. I don't think I was fully prepared to swallow the pill that people can make a mockery of the church while actually in it. Imagine my surprise when I started to take a closer look at televangelists. Everything I thought I knew about life up to that point all seemed so wrong, yet fit perfectly in a world that made wrong seem so right. The glamour of perception was sparkly. It didn't take much to catch on that most sparkly things came attached to expensive price tags. With that said I secretly reduced my level of the all-knowing to just about almost being a complete know-it-all, but according to the lyrics of one of my favorite popular R&B songs, "almost doesn't count." I needed money to pay for almost.

My first inclination was to strike it rich on stage, performing before masses of screaming adoring fans. I was only missing one thing – screaming adoring fans. That plan was over before it started. When I did the calculations in my head, though, sparkly things plus expensive price tags equaled one thing – retail! It made sense, so I did a few short stints as a cashier in a couple of Pentagon City Shopping Center store fronts. It paid some bills and filled my closet for a while but it still wasn't enough. I needed to think bigger. I needed to think outside of the box. And what a coincidence, a briefcase is a box! Television always glamorized men with briefcases. Everyone in the mid-90s knew that what was portrayed on television was some sense of the truth, so the guys on the tele obviously had to have enough money to afford the almost I was looking for. After all, briefcases weren't cheap. That's when I beefed up my resume (and by beefed up I mean lied) to land me a glamorous 9 to 5 job enveloped in a maze of cubicles, unknowing that office work was no more than the idea of turning tricks for a bunch of stiffs in a building who knew not your name. Don't get me wrong. I'm not saying I was an escort – at least not in a literal sense. On the streets of Office Politics, between Mail Room Lane and Cafeteria Court, all working class citizens are somebody's bitch waiting to be passed around to fill the requirements of the "other duties as assigned" not quite so plainly laid out in the employee handbook.

In the most facetious way possible, corporate America was a mere ho stroll where every worker got fucked one small paycheck at a time. A lesson I learned all too soon and still not soon enough.

When I took my first step into the land of office work, no one bothered to warn me of the dangers that lurked inside every manila folder. There, I was a virgin to data processing, mail pickups, and switchboard operations. Somehow I was convinced that all I had to do was show up at an office with a briefcase, a bright smile and a "yessum" attitude and by osmosis would receive a warm welcome, an employee of the month picture frame with my photo inside, and a corner office.

Boy, was I wrong.

Chapter 7

Lazy Heifer

Couch Potato Productions

Job Announcement

Position Title: Personal Flunky II

Company/Contact: Lazy Heifer Couch Potato Productions, Anywhere I Need You To Be, USA

Salary: Peanuts & Bubble Gum Wrappers

Closing Date: When the damn job is filled. Duh.

The Position: Flunky will scratch/kiss reporting supervisor's ass, jump on demand, and serve as personal flunky to CEO, CFO, President, Vice President, Assistant to the Assistant Administrative Assistant and Janitor of Lazy Heifer Couch Potato Productions.

Minimum Qualifications: One year of experience equivalent to jackass/dumbass or two years of experience equivalent to a nobody that's looking to be recognized for anything; a knock-off Bachelor's degree from a notable education by mail certificate program or one year experience as a milk crate packer. Full understanding that applicant will not speak unless spoken to, have no spine, no personal goals, no opinion, no friends, no life, no drama, and no chance of amounting to anything more than a talentless schmuck seeking approval from anyone who couldn't possibly give two shits less about them. Must be willing to rob banks and/or hold up liquor stores, work for peanuts, bubble gum, and saltine cracker crumbs. Must have strong feet or wheels on ankles (excessive walking required) and able to lift objects 15 lbs or greater (applicant will lift his/her ego, pride and self-worth off the floor frequently).

Special Selection Factors: Employment is contingent on the passing of a medical/physical examination and must be able to work weekends, rotating shifts, and holidays as required, commanded, demanded, and expected. Employment is contingent upon successful completion of a pre-employment alcohol/drug test. The test is to determine the presence of alcohol and/or illegal drugs, unauthorized prescription drugs.

Physical Abilities: Must be healthier than a dying willow tree; able to go without food and beverage for extended periods of time; and maintain a high level of low self-esteem.

Preference: Bilingual (English/Pig Latin/Ebonics) speaking skills.

Requirement: Physically unable to say "No."

How to Apply: Submit a professional resume (or something close to it) to:

Lazy Heifer Couch Potato Productions, 000 ½ N. Nowhere Street, 3rd Floor Basement, Anywhere I Need You To Be, USA 20101-0001

NO PHONE OR FAX SUBMISSIONS

*As a condition of employment, employees are required upon hire to sign a drug-free workplace agreement, though duties may include getting some green from nearby projects at employer's request.

*Following an offer of employment, and prior to starting work, individuals must have a pre-employment drug test by a physician designated by Lazy Heifer Couch Potato Productions. The examination will be paid for out of applicant's pocket (Cash only. Peanuts and bubble gum not accepted). Refusal or inability to pay for the exam will result in automatic disqualification of applicant consideration.

Note: If applicant has additional questions, please do not bother to ask. Employers of Lazy Heifer Couch Potato Productions do not care and will not listen. Hired applicant will serve LHCPP, not the other way around.

My corporate struggle began in the 3rd floor suite of Lazy Heifer Couch Potato Productions some winters back. It was my first year in college, as well as the first year of me living on my own. I was young and eager to prove my readiness for adulthood. Having graduated from a school of hard knocks (aka any high school in America), where the first curriculum standard was Competition 101, I thought that I could handle anything; until I met her. Angela Shapiro, Assistant to the Assistant Administrative Assistant for Not-To-Do Governmental Affairs. In our first meeting, she was as sweet as powdered donuts. Her words were soft; handshake firm; and eyes piercing. She wore a gray two piece pinstripe suit that stopped just below her knees, the stripes similar to the bars of a cell inside a women's midget correctional facility. All smiles with every word, Angela summed up the principles, policies, and expectations of the office while holding a clipboard firmly to her breast, checking off each notation cited as she oriented me to the job.

As any new employee would, I smiled and said "no problem" a lot. That seemed to earn me a few brownie points. Angela showed me to my office. It wasn't actually an office. It was a small desk inside a copier room beside the restrooms at the end of a long dark hallway away from the other workstations.

I called it an office because it made me sound more important to those of my friends that had no jobs.

As she took me on a tour of the office, she introduced me to my new colleagues. Some welcomed me with gracious smiles while others greeted me with a wave of a hand and the backs of their head. I wasn't completely surprised by the response. I'd witnessed all types of folks in my every day travels that were less than receptive. Some people, I accepted, are just shady by nature.

There were some workers that looked me up and down as if I clearly did not belong. A few people spoke with their eyes instead of their mouths. There was one guy that smelled like old coffee. Anyone that smells like old coffee, I thought, can't be good so I promised myself to keep an eye on him. There was also a woman who was kind of touchy-feely. Because I didn't know her, I kept the term "sexual harassment" in the back of my mind, even though her hands were admittedly soft and stimulated me in all the right places. I recall thinking she was either going to be my confidant or my downfall. Overall, for a first impression the people were okay.

The sound of my mother's voice echoed in my head, reciting what she deemed a necessary warning of the five basic senses needed to survive in an office setting: sight, sound, smell, touch, and taste. I can remember growing up as a child, Mama plopping on the couch after a long day of work with a cigarette in one hand and a glass of Tang in the other. She would tell me about her overbearing supervisor, her lazy compatriots, and the tasteless lunch she'd copped from the building's cafeteria. Her stories weren't always funny, but Mom had always been an animated woman. She regularly injected a lesson of the five elements of survival, particularly in regard to the office: Sight, because you've got to be able to spot bullshit a mile away; Sound, because people will talk a lot and say nothing at all. What they don't say are the things you want to hear; Smell, because people are quick like mice, so it's imperative that you are able to smell a rat; Touch, because everyone needs to know what it feels like to have a door slammed in their face; and finally Taste, because there is nothing sweeter than the taste of revenge and victory.

‡

Angela and I finished the office tour and finally returned to my desk. Upon it was a stack of folders, two dried out ink pens, a notepad, and a plastic bag for barfing. I was a little weirded out by the barf bag at first until I remembered Mama's voice saying,

"Working makes me sick." When I put two and two together, it all made sense. Before my ass touched the seat of the swivel chair, Angela's warm disposition shifted dramatically. Horns sprouted out of her head. Fangs grew from her mouth. A lightning bolt flashed before her and the room became dark enough to be confused with a midnight storm in a pumpkin patch. This bitch had turned into the devil.

"I really wish I had more time to stand here and familiarize you with the office but I have more important things to do." If I had a football in hand I would have been tackled by her words.

"If you look inside your desk, you'll find a few folders that need to be filed before lunch. I also need you to pick up the mail, turn in the rest of your paperwork to human resources, swab the deck, bait a hook, and gut a few fish, all before you pick up a couple cups of coffee for the directors from the corner bakery about sixteen blocks from here. There's also a staff meeting at eleven. Be prepared to introduce yourself."

With that she turned and slithered down the hall, leaving me up to my ears in being in way over my head. I hadn't been working for more than twenty minutes and already I wanted to pour salt on my first office enemy to see if she'd shrivel up like a slug. Before I knew it, my head was cradled in my arms upon the top of my desk when Lori Molligan, another employee at Lazy Heifer Couch Potato Productions, popped in.

"Ahem." Lori cleared her throat, interrupting what looked like me napping on the job. Naturally I jumped, startled. Slightly embarrassed for appearing to be a slacker, I rose to receive her.

"Hi. I didn't mean to disturb you. I can see you're busy. I just wanted to stop by and introduce myself." She extended her arm for a handshake. "I'm Lori Molligan, but you can call me Lori. I heard that the new employee was starting today and I know how rough the first day can be. If there's anything you need, let me know and I'll find someone to help you."

Lori was a relatively thin, fair skinned woman with huge knockers and a blond air about her. She smiled a lot and spoke volumes with her eyebrows. I sensed a small detection of nosiness about her instead of genuine warmth that a traditional first day welcoming brings. It was really too soon to tell considering she was only in my office for all of thirty seconds. Far be it from me to pass judgment.

"I remember my first day here. As a matter of fact, Angela gave me the office walk through. She's the nicest woman as long as you don't piss her off or know any more than she does. She gets threatened easily." She giggled as if she had said something funny.

Out of courtesy, I mustered up a generic laugh. After having a face-to-face with a devil incarnate, I thought it best to get on the good side of someone. Besides, Lori was kind of cute, aside from the pimples lined across her chin. She seemed like someone I wouldn't mind going to lunch with, even though the acne would probably ruin my appetite. She stood in a not so straight upright position, seemingly weighed down by her heavy boobs. I thought it refreshing to accidentally stare at her jugs on purpose. They took my attention away from her chin.

As she continued to talk, I continued to pretend to listen, unaware that time was slowly ticking away and I had yet to get started on the list of demands Angela left for me. What had I gotten myself into? In twenty minutes I had a run in with Satan, been groped, sized up, and left to drown in a sea of manila folders. "Welcome to an eternal loop of Monday," I thought.

This was probably the first time in my life that I understood why adults warned me not to be in such a rush to grow up. I never realized how good I had it. As a child my mother bought my food and clothes. She sent me to good schools and I never wanted for much of anything. But from the moment I hit adulthood, all responsibility landed on me: responsibility of my own words and actions; responsibility of my own bills; and now responsibility of becoming someone's bitch for hire. Day one as the assistant to the assistant of the Assistant Administrative Assistant for Not-To-Do Governmental Affairs was the day I vowed to become an expert in coming up with excuses to get out of work for a day.

As I sat behind my desk holding back tears (an instinctual reaction to my first experience of Monday blues), I grabbed one of the dried out ink pens that rested on the desk. There was no time like the present to jot down a few ideas of how I was going to get out of this mess. I had to think fast and think smart. Coming into an office full of working professionals put me at a disadvantage. I may not have been experienced enough to have a bunch of corporate lingo under my belt, but if there was anything I was good at, it was lying through my teeth (Thanks, Willy. Thanks, Bee).

After finally getting the pen to cooperate I wrote: DEAR SELF, TOMORROW WE WILL NEED TO TAKE A PERSONAL DAY OFF FROM WORK TO PREPARE FOR THE NEXT THIRTY YEARS OF PRE-RETIREMENT.

40 Arguably Good Excuses to Get Out of Work

According to a popular employment recruiting site, about 41% of hiring managers are suspicious of their employees' excuses for getting out of work. Outside of a common cold or minor car trouble, most excuses aren't believable, they say. I say "horse pucky!" What do they know? If life throws its highest cards at you while working for a stiff in an expensive suit, why the hell shouldn't you get a little creative with your excuses not to deal? Below are a few excuses that'll help you cut your days at the office in half. Feel free to use them at your leisure. Whether the excuse is believable or not is something the receiving ear has to take up with Human Resources and God.

1. My bangs fell out. I must go buy some synthetic tresses or either a pack of extra thick eye brow hair to cover my big ass forehead.
2. I'm renting a baby llama for my girlfriend's niece's best friend's business partner's cousin and I need to stay home to vacuum the constant poop from the foyer.
3. I got my private parts stuck in the zipper of my pants and need immediate medical attention.
4. At 3:00PM I've been scheduled to referee a pie fight between the Comcast and Verizon Fios

cable men, since they both think their cable services are the best. The loser will come in next week to make up the hours that I plan to miss today.
5. I ran over a squirrel while texting during an illegal street race with a blind man on a bike.
6. The goldfish that I flushed this morning stopped up the toilet and now my cup runneth over.
7. I have to go to the airport to pick up my French-Asian pen pal, Delicia Soo Wang.
8. My son beat up his teacher for taking his M&Ms during recess. The teacher threatened to have him expelled and now I have to go beat the bitch's ass, myself.
9. There is an embarrassingly foul odor coming from only one of my armpits and I am afraid to leave the house because the stench might kill the pigeons that built a nest over my garage door.
10. I'm getting my butt hairs braided at the African hair gallery after lunch and will not be returning to the office. Ever.
11. Today is the only day that I am available to read my daughter's diary.
12. Today is National I Don't Give a Fuck Day, and I don't give a fuck what you say, I will not be in the office.

13. I have a mandatory meeting with all the voices in my head and two bill collectors.
14. Someone told me that toenails can grow long enough to scrape the ground. Now that my toenails have finally grown to an unbelievable length, I'd like to test the theory out for myself.
15. My turrets syndrome of belching keeps flaring up.
16. I've been meaning to return the library book that I borrowed in the ninth grade. It's slightly overdue by about eighteen years.
17. I'm putting my great uncle in a rest home and I need to go visit his grave to see if he approves of the neighborhood the home is located in.
18. My boyfriend just broke up with me so now I have to slash all the tires on his skateboard, including the training wheels.
19. My Kotex string broke.
20. I have man cramps.
21. My neighbor's daughter swallowed my cat's hairball and now I have to take her to the vet to get a referral for a doctor.
22. I got laryngitis in my middle finger and will be unable to tell anyone to fuck off for three days.
23. My car flipped over six times before hurling over the rail of the 5th Street Bridge. I'm calling from the bottom of the ocean. I probably won't

be in tomorrow unless there is an express lane from Heaven that leads to the office.
24. My grandmother ran out of glaucoma medicine and I have to stand on the corner and try to hustle a hustler into giving me a stash on credit.
25. I have massive rug burns on my knees and am unable to walk. You'll have to get your own damn cup of coffee today!
26. I lost all my money playing bingo and now I don't have any change to get on the bus.
27. I'm stuck in the photo booth at Walmart.
28. The dog ate my car keys. My wife ate my car.
29. A booty call stole my alarm clock while I was in the bathroom coming up with a good excuse to be excused from work.
30. I can't find my shoes or my pet tarantula.
31. There is a busload of Jehovah's witnesses outside my door and I'm hiding under the couch until they go away. This may take a while.
32. With all the boiled eggs I ate this morning, I don't want shit to hit the fan.
33. My mother-in-law came to town for the weekend and got into a terrible accident. I have to take her to the hospital for emergency surgery to get the stick removed from her ass.

34. My wife's melons are sore from her recent breast implants. She needs me to stay home to massage them.
35. I won't be in the office today because I owe someone money and work is the first place they'll look for me. Oops! You're the one I owe money to.
36. After reviewing my last paycheck, I suddenly became claustrophobic.
37. Someone told me hard work doesn't guarantee a successful win so I'm not going to waste my time today.
38. I think my cocker spaniel caught an STD from the neighborhood bitch and needs to be taken to the puppy clinic to get tested.
39. I'm calling in blind cause I just don't see it happening today.
40. All my underwear has holes in them and I used the last bar of soap last night.

With the ink still scribbling across the note pad at rapid speed, a tall, dark woman with butt-length braided extensions appeared at the entry way of my office . . . ahem, workspace. She stood there for a few seconds allowing me to notice her. My first reaction was "What now?" until I accepted that a first day on any job is most likely filled with more introductions than actual work. She wasn't exactly a pretty woman, but she did elude a certain kind of back alley charm that I was more used to than any work environment. The kind of alley where ice cream trucks jingle their bells to the tune of one of Snoop Dog's pop culture chorus lines long after the street lights have come on. She wore all purple with heavy eye makeup to match. Her fingernails were long and sharp like my cat's claws just before his grooming appointment. Finally, someone I can relate to!

"Hey baby."

Her name was Bertha Bennett, the most desired secretary on the 3rd floor. Angela mentioned Bertha's name a few times during our orientation, recognizing her as a great resource for anything that I'd need. It was nice to put a face with a name though she wasn't quite what I expected. Bertha looked like a cross between an eggplant and a Ziploc bag full of seedless grapes.

"Angela asked me to come over and introduce myself to you. I'm Bertha. I work in the executive suite just down the hall." Instead of reaching out for a friendly handshake she embraced me tightly. I almost died a little from the suffocation of her clench. She continued. "If you need anything at all, don't hesitate to ask me." There was a high level of comfort that I felt with her, almost as if I'd known her my whole life. Well, more like twenty minutes rather than twenty years but a long twenty minutes.

"Actually, Angela left me a pretty intense list of things to do before the morning staff meeting. She said something about gutting some fish and picking up a cup of coffee from the next town a few hundred miles over." Bertha exploded with a maddening raspy laugh. It was irritating enough to be fine with never hearing it again.

"I like you." she responded. "I think you and I are going to get along just fine."

"You're not going to hug me again, are you?" I felt I needed to brace myself for another set of broken bones.

"Maybe later. What I will do is walk with you to get that coffee. Come on."

We left the building and walked what seemed to be a million baby steps to a quaint little corner bakery run by a family of Africans sixteen blocks away from the office, just as Angela said. In that time, she and I had gotten to know each other a little bit. I gave her the cliché run down of my life post high school and pre-employment. She told me about her six kids, two goldfish, and what foods to avoid in the cafeteria on Wednesdays. As we waited for the directors' coffees to be prepared we continued our chat inside a window booth over a couple of chocolate glazed, macadamia donuts. The inexperienced reporter in me began probing her to get a feel for her thoughts on the office and the people in it.

While she delved deeper into prose, I'd almost forgotten I was talking to an office manager and instead envisioned her in hooker heels and queen-sized ripped stockings. She referred to herself in third person a few times and had names for her breasts. Her favorite words were "bitch" and "boo boo" and each seemed to roll off her lips with the mention of Mr. Roswell and Mr. Dunning, the co-executive chiefs of Lazy Heifer Couch Potato Productions.

"They are nice men," she said. "They just ask for a lot and always put me in awkward positions. I keep saying I'm not going to take their demands lying down but I usually swallow my pride. By the time I'm finished polishing something off, I'm too tired to stand up for myself."

I couldn't help but wonder if we were still talking about the office. Her words reminded me of a little old whore house in Texas.

"Why do you let them ride you like that?" I asked.

"I need the money, Boo Boo. Times are hard and I have a bunch of mouths to feed."

Obviously, I was becoming more interested in the conversation. She gave me some juicy information about the office while offering a lot of inappropriate information about herself. What more could a guy ask for?

Bertha described her days as never being easy. She said they were filled with the typical functions of a secretary – answering phones, scheduling meetings, and stroking egos. Her duties didn't end with taking care of merely the two executives. She was the madam of them all. Everyone went to her with their needs. She was often specially requested by the other department heads when it came time for a job fulfillment that their respective secretaries couldn't handle, which of course didn't always sit well with the other secretaries. To them Bertha raised the bar on the level of progress among the support staff. She was sort of like the head hooker on the stroll, grabbing all the business from the other girls. Like every dog that gets tired of chasing a bone, she was very convincing at having everything under control; though she admitted to sometimes finding a need to stick her head out of a window to catch her breath. "Working like a dog," she said, "makes a bitch tired." This was perhaps the second most important lesson I learned about working – the first lesson, of course, being how to come up with a winning excuse to get out of work.

She went on to explain the behaviors of some of the colleagues in the office, focusing heavily on the conduct of Mr. Roswell and Mr. Dunning. Being the slave drivers that they were, rest was a concept Bertha was not all too familiar with. According to her, Roswell and Dunning ran the office like a well-oiled machine, each employee acting as a bolt that holds some major part of the machine together with another. Both executives were adamant about keeping peace among their workers. Keeping Bertha available to support all of her needy coworkers is what seemed to keep everyone happy; everyone except her.

According to her, from nine until noon she posted herself at the front desk, flashing a scarlet red sticky pad to any director looking for her to perform some type of duty with a done-right-the-first-time finish. She later described herself as a receptacle for everybody's stuff. It sounded like a dirty job, but I guess someone had to do it.

"How did you get into this line of work? I mean surely you wanted to do something else with your life." Things got interesting with her response.

"I was young, just like you," she said. "I had just moved here from Wyoming and needed some steady cash. It gets awfully cold hopping from one unemployment line to another. Working the corners probably would have brought in some quick cash but also a lot of other things I definitely didn't want. I figured that I'd stand a better chance of getting fucked in an office than I would behind a taco stand. I heard Roswell and Dunning were looking for a gal to sit pretty at the head of their office. I came in for an interview, had a couple of callbacks, and the rest is history. I've been under them ever since."

"So you like it here?"

"Boo Boo, whether I like it or not is not even important. A girl's got to do what a girl's got to do."

"Le café est prêt!" The French speaking bakery owner interrupted our engrossing conversation to alert us our order was ready, giving us just enough time to return to the office for the morning staff meeting.

It goes without saying that I was not looking forward to the meeting for a number of reasons. First and foremost, I wasn't anxious to see Angela again. After seeing devil horns grow from the sides of her head, I was kind of scared of her. And by kind of I mean deathly. She reminded me of all the sins that I'd committed that I tried so hard to forget about in hopes that St. Peter would one day accept my admittance ticket to the gates of heaven. Secondly, I wasn't looking forward to introducing myself to a room full of people whom I didn't know. Even as a kid, I hated showing up on the first day to a new school for fear that the teacher would make me tell the class who I was. The rush of the staff meeting had no different effect on the butterflies fluttering inside my stomach. I could imagine a bunch of eyes locked on me, analyzing every one of my words. Their stares piercing through me like a pack of safety pins. Lastly, I just didn't want to go. Something about the words "staff meeting" sounded boring. Actually, anything with the word "meeting" in it sounds boring, unless – of course – one is referring to meeting a blind date for the first time. That's not boring. That's another kind of feeling all together – something along the lines of fear.

How to Spice Up a
Boring Office Staff Meeting

Are your staff meetings a major snooze fest? Of course they are, but they don't have to be. After all, what's an office without a little humor – excluding the office jerk you love to gossip about and laugh at? Although it's true that no business will ever be successful without a few hundred meetings per week, there's no reason why you can't have fun while hoping your ears fall off while you listen to a long list of agenda items that have absolutely nothing to do with your particular load of work.

Here are a few ideas to help spruce things up the next time your director calls an all-hands staff meeting. Keep in mind that some of your colleagues may not have the same kind of warped sense of humor as you do. Most of them probably have no sense of humor at all which will make these ideas all the more enjoyable for you. Let's begin, shall we?

- The proper way to start off any meeting is to call attention to yourself. The best way to do that is to compliment your supervisor in reverse. If you don't have anything nice to say to or about your boss, say it anyway. You're opinion and honesty will either be appreciated or reprimanded. Either way it will never be forgotten. You might be forgotten after you've been fired and therefore relieved from any further staff meetings but your comment will live on forever. It may however come back to bite you in the ass when you're in need of a reference for your next job.

- If the reverse compliments turn out to be duds, grab your neighbor by the chin and French kiss them passionately. Hold your breath just in case that neighbor's breath smells like something crawled inside their mouth and died. Be aware that you may develop some sort of reputation. However, as in the case with the reverse compliments, you may not be employed long enough to care, so it's all good.

- It's always appreciated when you are an active participant in a meeting. Sleeping is usually frowned upon as a legitimate form of participation. Don't ask me why. As many times as I've done it, no one seems to like it so just take my word for it. If you can't get away with catching some Zs on company time, try offering a few suggestions to change a policy or two. A suggestion that would really get the conversation going would be to replace the water in all the water coolers with vodka. Your suggestion would

be more effective if you are intoxicated at the time of your proposal.
- While you are drunk, there would be no better time to discuss your pay scale among the group. A few people may consider this inappropriate because it's kind of difficult to understand slurred speech. Since inhibitions are lowered when one is inebriated, what should you care? What better time to inquire about your impending pay raise, especially if you know you are overqualified and underpaid for the job you perform after you have exhausted all of your spare time playing internet games? A drunken rant at a staff meeting is the perfect place to voice your concerns.

These ideas may have you ejected from the meeting, even more likely from the building in its entirety. If so, then you have succeeded in the quest to liven things up. There's one very important rule that you must never forget when going the extra mile to make your meeting a little more interesting. That rule is: "Nobody likes a quitter!" Once you've been escorted out of the building by security or chased by a hoard of disgruntled employees, don't let that be the last time they see you. After escaping the clutches of the law or after you've healed from the beat down your colleagues will have given you behind the break room soda machine, return to the office as if nothing happened. You must though expect the colleagues not to be too pleased with your return, given the circumstances by which you left.

Your homecoming is not promised to be easy. Because everyone in the organization will be afraid you've returned to stir up more trouble, all of the doors will be blocked with people waiting to gun you down with loaded staplers. The organization may possibly beef up security by renting man-eating shiatsus to attack you on sight. If, by chance, you have managed to slip into the building unnoticed and are somehow discovered by someone, make note of all unlocked windows to jump out of in case you end up being chased again. Don't exit the building without releasing the most explosive fart your ass can muster up! Making such a dramatic exit will surely give the office something to remember and talk about for many more staff meetings to come.

If you stick to these guidelines, I guarantee you will never have to worry about another dull staff meeting again. Some of the ideas may be farfetched, but what fun is life without a little spontaneity?

‡

The meeting began with a few thousand paragraphs of shop talk. I sat at the opposite end of the table from executive chief Vince Roswell. Beside him sat co-executive, Dick Dunning. The discussion of practical procedures for the department's latest project implementation bounced back and forth across the room. The only things that were missing were a couple of tennis rackets, and Venus and Serena Williams. Much like the game of tennis, I didn't know what the hell was going on. No matter to me. The time gave me a chance to come up with a winning self-introduction. The butterflies in my stomach morphed into baby dragons. My bladder was shrinking and my throat was dryer than an Angola desert. Bertha sat on my left side in direct view of Angela. Lori sat two seats away from her. She looked just as bored as I was. Ironically at the exact moment that I wondered what she was thinking, I swear I heard a cricket in the room. That broke my concentration. The irony of a cricket and an airhead was much funnier than me stumbling over my words.

Under the table, Bertha bumped my leg with her knee. With her elbow planted firmly atop a white sheet of paper on the tabletop, she slid me a note. Unnoticed, I read the scribbled message: WATCH OUT FOR HER.

I replied with a raised eyebrow.

"Angela," Mr. Roswell, a tall thin man with a bald spot on both sides of his head took the floor. "Why don't you introduce our new employee to the staff?"

Mr. Roswell's request lassoed her. She looked irritated and constipated at the same time. Her horns weren't as evident as they were in my office and her smile was almost as sincere as it was before her Gemini twin snatched her personality and went all "Angela has left the building."

"Why don't we let him introduce himself?" Her response was coarsely pleasant.

Is this what Bertha's note meant? I wanted to take my ink pen and write the words SHUT UP on her forehead. Thankfully Bertha came to my rescue.

"Mr. Roswell, if you don't mind, this is Mr. IfITold YouHisName IdHaveToKillYou, but he goes by Hottywood." Bertha's glorifying introduction continued. She soaked up the attention like a sponge, introducing me to the staff as if I was a recipient of an Academy award. I was just as much in awe of myself as was everyone else in the room. I didn't even know I did half the shit Bertha said I'd done. Whether or not she made up the story to make me sound better than clever, it was stellar! Thanks, Bertha!

The staff received me openly and quickly. All of the focus slowly shifted back to the practical procedures – all but Angela's. Her focus remained on Bertha and I. If her stare were a ninja, it would have killed, much like every hurled ninja star to the heart or every snap, back, side and round house kick to the temple as seen in every martial arts flick ever made. On the street, I probably would have asked her what it was she was looking at (you know, if she weren't a ninja), but this wasn't about me. Her eyes butted heads with Bertha's cold stare. Neither woman flinched. Bertha's claws were just as sharp as Angela's. It was a tug of war of no blinking between the two. You could cut the tension with a pitch fork. I saw the same horns growing from Bertha's head as I did Angela's. The room had gone black. Everyone else had disappeared except Angela and Bertha standing on the center of the conference room table with a spotlight shining on them, and me sitting on the dark sideline with a bag of Martin's sour cream and onion potato chips in one hand and a white, foam cup filled with Pepsi in the other. About forty minutes passed between the beginning and end of the battle of the broads. Neither of them emerged a victor and I had crumbs all over my chest.

After the meeting, like mice, everyone scattered. Angela slithered down the hall, leaving a light trail of shed serpent skin. If there were any more steam seeping from her ears I could have tossed her on a train track and rode her ass to Birmingham.

Curiosity fueled me. I half way wanted to guess what the beef was about before confirming any actual suspicions with Bertha.

Dear Hottywood,

I overheard a couple of my coworkers talking about me and my poor work performance. Should I confront them about it or continue to act normally?

Water Cooler Rumors

Dear Water Cooler Rumors,

It's never a good thing when you overhear someone talking negatively about you. The first thing any average person wants to do is smear Vaseline over their face and go all WWE on a mofo (codename for motherfucker)! As much fun as drop-kicking someone sounds, I wouldn't advise that during normal business hours. Save the violence for a staff field trip to an after five happy hours joint.

Let me be serious with you for a second before I drop you the 4-1-1 on the Hottywood revenge tip. You have to be careful if you plan on confronting anyone about badmouthing you behind your back. They may have legitimate reasons. Acting a fool would only add credibility to their whispers. The last thing you need is for more coworkers, especially upper level management, to see your flaws.

What I would suggest is that you evaluate your own performance. If you are screwing up, getting your shit together would be its own just reward and will also keep you employed. If you work for the federal government, then advising you to work harder, better or smarter is sufficient enough advice equivalent to advice that I would give if I were speaking to a brick wall, so kicking somebody's ass at happy hour will more than likely solve all of your problems. Now here are a few innovative ideas that will help you to get back at that those bagel eating gossipers:

1. Replace all the coffee beans in the break room with stale, decaf coffee beans. Everyone in the office will be sluggish for the entire day and won't know why. By doing this, all of your colleagues will appear to be lazy and unenthused. Somewhere down the line, you can use their slothfulness against them. The key here is to think big in small steps.
2. Every time your coworkers leave the office, remove the white paper from their printers and replace them with pages from a Playboy magazine. This way they'll be terminated for harboring porn in the office.
3. Using a black magic marker, scratch the names off of all incoming faxes. If no one knows who

the recipients are, the faxes will be discarded, the issues will never get resolved, and your coworkers will be questioned for their lack of performance.
4. Hire a gang of obese, gypsy belly dancers to beat them up in the parking lot and post the whole episode on YouTube. You'll get nothing out of this, but it sure as hell would be fun to watch.

If your associates are covertly trying to bring you down, then you shouldn't go down without a fight and you shouldn't go down alone. If somehow there is a pink slip involved with your name written all over it, then you have nothing to lose with getting even. If, on the other hand, you want to take the high road, get your act together and stop giving them shit to talk about.

Check back with me to let me know how things work out for you. And if you decide to take me up on that whole YouTube idea, make sure you give me a link so I'll know where to look! Good luck.

Bertha and I convened in the cafeteria. This was my chance to get some answers to the questions left unanswered from the staff meeting. The dining hall was abuzz with caffeine-pumped employees. Scattered around the room were stiffs in khaki pants and starched shirts, and ladies wearing grandma pumps. Bertha and I sat at a small table in the corner at the far end of the room, away from the majority of the people. The rest of our department staff, including Angela, sat at a large table in the center of the dining hall. I had a perfect view of the assistant to the assistant. Bertha's back side faced Angela.

"So Bertha, what the hell was all that about?" There was no time for buttering bread. I wanted to get to the root of the stare down. "It was like watching you and Angela box with your eyes."

Bertha snickered and bit into her already half eaten burger. A combination of tomato juice and mayonnaise trickled down the corner of her mouth. She chewed her food thirty-two times before swallowing and taking a swig of her root beer. I couldn't help but look at my watch impatiently, wondering if she was going to answer my question any time before lunch was over.

"That Angela is a bitch. We had it out a couple of months ago over a letter that she'd written to the executives complaining about work load and some other bullshit." I could feel Bertha's adrenaline rush as she explained her aversion for Angela. Her eye brows curled and her nostrils flared. She looked like she was ready to get up and pour mustard all over Angela's suit, which personally would have amused me, but she maintained her cool and continued.

"After giving the letter to management, she told them that I was the one who wrote it." She took another bite of her sandwich, giving me the perfect opportunity to respond with follow up questions.

"Were you the one that wrote the letter? What did it say? Did you get in trouble?" With all the questions that spilled out of my mouth, I could have applied for a job as a cross examining attorney instead of an entry level general service officer who doubled as an assistant assistant to an assistant. Speaking with a mouth full of food she replied while spewing crumbs in my direction. "No, I didn't write the letter! The bitch lied on me. In fact, I happen to have a copy of it here in my purse. I keep it with me to remind me to smack myself in the forehead every time I get an urge to be nice to her."

Rummaging through her oversized handbag she pulled out a folded sheet of paper. Glancing at the page, the word MEMORANDUM jumped out in big bold letters. I read silently, giggled a little, and gasped a lot as I stole a few peeps at Angela. The memo read as follows:

MEMORANDUM

TO: Senior Management

FROM: All Employees

SUBJECT: Employee Grievance

I think enough of my hair has fallen out for me to finally feel comfortable enough to tell you that I am overworked and stressed out! Between the thousands of phone calls, emails, and unexpected deadlines, not to mention taking on the responsibilities of those employees who have been fired, are out sick, or simply too overwhelmed to complete their own assignments, I must admit that I rather like my hair and want to keep it just a little while longer before old age takes the privilege away from me.

As if coming to work every day isn't hard enough, especially after having dealing with the hard blows of life (i.e., running out of cheap liquor and not being able to replenish because the liquor store closed ten minutes early; disobedient kids; untrained pets; hard-ball bill collectors, and nosey neighbors),

I have to come into the office and fall behind in my workload to attend three-hour staff meetings and sit through meetings to discuss what's going to be discussed in the next meeting.

While my colleagues are freely attending extended two-hour lunches, I have approximately twenty-two minutes to eat, digest and shit before the next emergency arises and my ulcer erupts – again. The bags under my eyes, heavy from lack of sleep, carry a load of nervous tension that causes me to twitch uncontrollably when I hear the heels of your shoes escalating toward the invisible door of my cubicle. Hiding for the sake of sanity is my first inclination. However, there's no time permitted on my calendar, as poking my eyeballs out with a #2 pencil has taken up all of what's left of my no-minute coffee break.

I am not writing this letter to complain about the two hundred percent increase in my work load, the inconsideration of needy coworkers that only come to me when they require something while ironically forgetting my name, or the fact that the cafeteria serves yesterday's coffee every day and always seems to run out of sugar whenever I finally find the energy to drag my ass to the coffee pot. I am writing this letter to ask for your help. Help me to understand why my outstanding performance evaluation has omitted me from getting either a change in job title or a pay increase to match the duties I've collected since the last five to seven employees left the company. Help me to understand why our department rests on the top floor when studies show that people inflicted with heavy amounts of stress are inclined to jump out of windows in hopes to land in the middle of a busy intersection. Help me to understand why kudos are given to Jane and John when I'm the one scarred from drafting proposals, memos, charts, graphs, and PowerPoint presentations.

Even now, as I write this letter, I must cut my time short because I only have thirty-seven seconds left to run to the bathroom and get to the meeting I've only been invited to because I'm needed to carry the heavy box of reports that's going to be distributed to the rest of the team.

It's not that I don't love my job, because I do. I just want to live long enough to enjoy it and buy the donuts that my small paychecks can only afford. You guys are killing me slowly, so I implore your help! Hire a temp; build another me out of match sticks and Elmer's glue. Hell, I don't care! But pretty soon there's not going to be enough of me to go around because I'll be buried somewhere six feet under a pile of manila folders.

Sincerely,

Your most humble, gracious and dedicated employee with only a half head of hair.

P.S.

You have a call on line #2.

‡

I couldn't contain my laughter. The contents of the memo absolutely seemed like something Bertha would say given the short amount of time I'd known her. However, her irritated expression disagreed with my assumption. I couldn't believe anyone would write such a thing, let alone submit it to anyone for official review. Bertha, on the other hand, didn't have a same grip on the humor as I did. With insistent reluctance, she turned to stab Angela with another sharp gawk. What she didn't expect was for Angela to migrate over to our table for a verbal confrontation, no doubt as cold as the silent confrontation as in the earlier staff meeting.

"Ahem. Is there a problem?"

Angela spoke with authority. If she were out on the street, she would more than likely be pulling off her earrings. Bertha took another bite of her burger. She took her time as she chewed and gathered her thoughts. Her eyes never left mine. She grabbed the napkin that lay in her lap and wiped her hands, followed by another swig of soda.

"Angela, Boo Boo, the only problem I have right now is you. Do you want to help me solve it or do you want to carry your skinny ass back over to that table and mind your own business?"

Bertha clearly had no problem speaking her mind. After making her rebuttal, she tossed her napkin on the table and shifted her body to face Angela.

"I don't think it is appropriate behavior for you to discuss me behind my back. It looks like you are entertaining the new help at my expense."

"Help?!" I blurted. Oh, no she didn't!

"Honey," Bertha shot back, "one, what I do on my lunch break and with whom is none of your damn business. Two, you don't know what the hell I'm talking about, so as far I'm concerned you need to go somewhere and work on your insecurity issues. And, three, I suggest you lower that bass in your voice unless you really want to find out how much of a problem I have with you. Now, is there anything else you want to discuss or do we need to step outside and handle this like men?"

Angela's face turned pink. She was pissed and there was no hiding it. I have to give it to her, though, she stood her ground. She had a lot of nerve to approach Bertha the way she did. Bertha didn't exactly look like someone you'd want to rub the wrong way. If she wasn't from the streets, she looked enough like it to keep on her good side.

"Bertha, I don't know what your deal is but you are not setting a good example for anyone, including yourself."

"Bitch!" Bertha interrupted but Angela refused to let her intercept.

"Like I said, your behavior is highly inappropriate and I don't appreciate it. And just to let you in on a little secret, Miss Hood Rat Barbie, this isn't over."

Bertha stood face to face with Angela. "Now that I'm in your face, you want to repeat that?"

"What's the matter, Bertha? Are my words too big for you to understand?" I slid my chair back because I sensed that things were going to take a violent turn and I didn't want either of these broads to knock my

French fries on the floor. I didn't know whose side to take. Bertha seemed to have been in my corner from the moment we met, but I was kind of turned on by Angela's backbone. She must have been raised around some black folks because she stood her ground just as firmly as the ghettolicious Bertha. Angela flashed a cocky smile. She looked Bertha up and down and blatantly turned her back, flinging her hair like one of Charlie's Angels. Grains of dandruff released from the toss. I grabbed Bertha's arm in a fake attempt to stop her from swinging. My grip was not strong at all. I secretly yearned for a good chick fight, like any normal man would. As Angela walked away she turned and spoke one final word.

"If I were you, I'd be careful of the company I keep, Mr. Hottywood. Bertha isn't as sweet as the pie she looks like she's eaten." Another bolt of lightning flashed in the sky with her departing words. She showed no signs of fear or weakness. She was ready for anything Bertha dished. She may have been hard core like Bertha, but unlike the giant California raisin from Wyoming, she kept her calm. It was like having really good seats at a live taping of "Mean Girls" with knock offs of Lindsay Lohan and Rachel McAdams.

"Are you okay?" I knew the question was dumb. Bertha was obviously not okay. But what else could I say to break the ice?

"I'm going to get that bitch. You watch. I'm going to catch her ass on a quiet street and beat the shit out of her. She done barked up the wrong tree. I'm just waiting for the right time."

All eyes in the cafeteria were glued to our table. Even the kitchen staff abandoned their grills to witness the commotion. The colleagues from our department didn't say a word. When Angela returned to her table, the lunch time chatter continued as if it never ended. The rest of the diners in the room whispered of the scene amongst themselves. Clearly the two women were the talk of the noon day crowd. I needed to pee but I was too afraid to leave Bertha by herself. As angry as she was, there was no telling what she was capable of doing. I just hoped she wouldn't wait until I finally decided to go to the bathroom to do it.

If I didn't say it before, or even if I have, "Welcome to corporate America."

‡

Office Gripes:
What's Not Written in the Employee Manual

Work, no matter if you love it or hate it, is never an easy place to be or an easy thing to do, but if you understand how it operates, then you can deal with it. Getting a paycheck every eighty hours isn't such a bad thing either – which in fact, is the part that everyone loves. On the other hand, no one knows all the little details that come with the package when they sign on to a new job.

Since work is the one place the average person spends most of his time, there are a few things about it that you need to know. First of all, what is work? Work is a place where you go to do a lot of things that you don't want to do for a bunch of people that you don't want to be around all day long. Some would argue that's no different than family, and in a sense that's true. An employee knows his coworkers just as well as he knows his relatives. The difference between work and family, though, is that you are paid to be a part of one group, but not the other.

I'm not going to spend a lot of time explaining to you why we work. To sum that up quickly, if we don't work, we don't eat. Everyone has to work to earn their keep. That theory dates all the way back to the caveman; and if you don't believe me, then you can go back in time and see for yourself. What I am going to explain to you is the minor technicalities that are overlooked at the office that easily turn a good day bad. Because I know you have about five minutes left in your fifteen minute break, I'm going to keep this list short. Perhaps by the time you finish reading it, you'll be more inclined to chuckle rather than make daggers out of pencil tips and envelope glue.

Skipping over the blah-blahs of the office's silly rules and policies, today we are going to discuss what's not written in the employee manual that you should be prepared for:

- **Coworkers may stand outside of an employee's office or cubicle and hold a conversation, without including the employee whose space is being violated.** Three thoughts come to mind: (A) Can you be any more rude? (B) Who cares? (C) See (A).
- **Coworkers may hold their entire telephone conversation on speaker phone.** Three thoughts come to mind: (A) Can you be any more rude? (B) Who cares? (C) See (A).
- **Any meeting is subject to begin before 10AM.** Let's be honest here. Who the hell can concentrate

before 10AM? Nothing in the world should be that important. After fussing with the cafeteria lady for not brewing a fresh pot of coffee, asking anyone to do anything except breathe is asking too much! Where is the compassion?

- **Staff meetings may run well over and into the lunch hour.** If you want an employee to work hard, you have to feed him. Food is the battery that keeps the body working properly. No one should feel as if they're working in a Chinese sweat shop (trust me, it's not fun). The bottom line is, any time a stomach growls louder than anyone can speak, it's time to end the damn meeting.
- **Brown bag lunch meetings are occasional requirements.** Epic violation of the employee manual. Somewhere written in the bylaws is a clause that awards an employee a full hour of personal time (thirty minutes for lunch and two fifteen minute breaks: Triple that if you work for the government). Dear supervisors and all those alike: The words "brown bag meeting" are fighting words!
- **Some employees may become too overwhelmed to complete their own work assignments without assistance.** Seriously? The finger should be pointed at management for not hiring people

with better time management skills. Management should look into time management courses for their staff development retreats. Management should also have its ass kicked for not warning employees that the phrase, "...and all other duties assigned," means doing someone else's job.

- **Employers may wait until an employment performance review to enlighten the employee on all of his/her screw ups.** I'm going to say this and leave it alone: You don't throw a brick at someone without telling them to duck if you don't have any intentions to hurt them.
- **The cafeteria is subject to run out of caffeinated coffee at any given time.** When it comes to dealing with certain demands, expectations, and the performance of miraculous feats, caffeine is the sedative dart that keeps the peace in a brood of animals. No coffee ranks up there with brown bag lunches in the category of "Fighting Words."
- **Unfortunately there is no liquor in the vending machines.** I don't think management or Congress will ever go for this, but you have to admit that stocking a vending machine with vodka miniatures is a pretty good idea. It would help everyone to take some of the edge off, unless of course, you're some sort of alcoholic. Hey, I

didn't say it was a perfect idea. There are some kinks that still need to be worked out.

- **Two or more employees may take a dump in the bathroom at the same time.** The one thing that two or more people should never share is shit.

‡

Over the course of the next few days, tension remained thick between Angela and Bertha. Because I sat at the end of the hall where I was the only living thing, not counting the dying plant that someone left on my desk as an office warming gift, I couldn't make out too much of their interaction. I could, however, see them trying extra hard to avoid one another whenever they passed in the hall.

The following days were even less exciting than the last. Angela's list of demands increased. I found myself doing a bunch of stuff that wasn't clearly defined by my job description. The phones never stopped ringing. I attended more meetings in a day than a day has hours. I also developed a small family of blisters on the bottom of my feet from walking to the corner bakery. I wasn't as satisfied with trading greasy carryout bags for a briefcase as I thought I would be. Living a corporate life appeared to be way more glamorous on television. I may not have once understood why Mama came home every day from a long day's work in a foul mood, but after having endured the brunt of high demands for low pay, I was beginning to catch on.

☦

Lori had been spending a considerable amount of time in my office. Her time spent with me was filled with personal questions – everything from my education to my blood type. I was slightly offended by the first hundred questions at first. However, after spending hours alone in a room with nothing but the sound of humming copier machines, I rather enjoyed the company. I think.

Still, her probing only confirmed my initial perception of her as a snoop. I seemingly found a guilty pleasure in lying to her about everything she asked about. I didn't get anything out of it. It was just fun. Snoop or not, I appreciated her presence because it came in handy when the sticky pads failed to keep my eyelashes attached to my eyebrows. While I sat on the fence with her journalistic approach to my personal business, she managed to keep me moderately entertained with the juicy gossip she provided regarding all of the office's associates.

According to her, rumor had it that Mr. Roswell and Mr. Dunning were more than just business partners. They and their wives were actually swingers that got together regularly to swap body juices. She said that whenever the wives arrived at the office at the same time, it was for a joint, daytime quickie. There were even times when Roswell and Dunning had a few closed door meetings without the wives.

Lori went further into the lives of every workmate until she finally came down to none other than Angela and Bertha. Word was Angela was initially in line for Bertha's job. She'd been working with Roswell and Dunning much longer than Bertha and could not fathom the thought of someone else getting that position, especially because she was the one running the office before Bertha was hired. When Bertha came along, the co-executives seemed to be more impressed with her assets than her credentials. They delegated Angela as the one to check Bertha's references, resulting in negative responses from the two and a half employers Bertha previously worked for. Those responses had greatly to do with her attitude and sometimes unprofessional manner of dress. Sadly for Angela, that was the selling point for Bertha. When Bertha came into the mix, she participated in a lot of the closed door meetings with Roswell and Dunning. She also had a better rapport with their wives. Some would argue that Bertha screwed her way to the top of the bottom of the totem pole. In the end, the only person that got screwed was Angela. She never healed from the bruise of having her job snatched from beneath her, which further explained why their squabble was so intense.

As Lori continued to relentlessly put everyone on blast, I couldn't help but feel flushed with apprehension. How in the hell did this woman know everybody's business? Surely the same way she was getting mine. She asked. Lori was a covert snitch, much like Sister Gabby Gossip from old Holy Hood Church of Mount Mattress Bedside Tabernacle. I thought to myself that she had a lot of nerve spreading the unholy word to me, someone she barely knew. With a strong intent to divert the subject, I inquired further about the mysterious memo that had Angela and Bertha's shorts so much in a bunch.

"Lori," I began. "What's the deal with this memo that's stamped with Bertha's name? I mean, Bertha told me what it was about, but whatever came from it?"

"You haven't read the last page of your employee manual, have you?" She was delighted to entertain my query. She got me. I was guilty of not reading the manual. Who reads those, anyway? It's not like an Agatha Christie novel or even an InTouch magazine, for that matter. Whatever the case, Lori specifically called the book by name so it must have held the answer to my question. Without hesitation, I grabbed the manual from underneath the leg of my wobbly desk. Quickly, I flipped to the end. I probably would have appreciated it if Lori had just told me what the result of the memo madness was, but after reading what I read I don't think she or anyone else could have summed it up any better than the words printed on the final page of the handbook.

MEMORANDUM

TO: All Employees

FROM: Senior Management

DATE: NOW!

SUBJECT: Fed Up!

To all fellow staff, though it is normal propaganda for management to send you correspondence to praise you for your continued hard work and commitment to the team, sadly we must bear the news of informing you that this is not that type of notice.

It has become apparent that some of you are unhappy with your current positions. Although some sympathy may be warranted, an executive decision has been made to collectively tell you all to get over yourselves.

For a little more than minimum wage you are expected to fulfill the duties required to execute all assigned projects either in a timely manner or within any preposterous time frame we see fit. With all of the busy work that we give you to keep you out of our hair, we are certain that you have no more time to complain than we do to care.

When we give you tasks as simple as sending "Thank You" cards to the group of strippers that showcase their nipple pasties at our annual Christmas party, or clean up leftovers from luncheons you aren't invited to, we are simply exercising our right to do what we are paid the big bucks to do – delegate – and not care about your disposable feelings.

You are obligated to comply with our needs and the needs we tell you are best for this company as in accordance with your Employee Manual, Article 256 Section 3-CII [pg. 781].

Effective Immediately:

- We will no longer praise you for the duties you are compensated to perform.
- All privileges of extended lunch breaks, personal calls (which are by default routed to the Employment Management Review [EMR] committee), and internet access (to include any form of chat sessions, Craigslist, YouTube, Facebook and Twitter) are banned.
- Toleration of your lack of initiative, poor body odor, profane language and uncoordinated outfits will hereby desist.
- All personal jealousies and bitterness are prohibited on company time.

- Any spoken word of noncompliance, disapproval or discernment with what you are told to do by any member of senior staff or anyone holding an interim position of like authority will result in immediate termination.

Any objections to these policies should be discussed with the personnel officer designated to put the final stamp on your pink slip.

Respectfully,

Management

cc:

Office of Personnel Division

The President of the United States of America

God

My eyes widened with each word. I didn't know whether to burst out in boisterous laughter or pack my bags and run for the hills.

"Does that answer your question?" Lori asked. I didn't know how to respond. Now I understood why Bertha was so upset.

"Oh, my goodness," I replied. "Ain't that some shit? But what I still don't understand is how Angela knew Bertha wrote the memo? And how did she get her hands on it to pass it on to management?" Things weren't adding up, until…

"Can you keep a secret?" Lori leaned in close, her décolletage pressing firmly against my forearm.

"If I can't keep a secret, there ain't a cow in Texas!" I had no idea what I was in store for.

"Angela wasn't the only one up for Bertha's job. I applied for it, too. I knew there was a 30/70 chance that I'd get it, so I took matters into my own hands. Having known the scoop about Roswell and Dunning, I decided to get a little closer to their wives. I conveniently ran into them in the elevator after one of their trysts. After striking up a conversation and flashing my melons, one thing led to another. Eventually the three of us had a few rendezvous of our own, sans their husbands. Each time, they promised me that I would be the one to land the job if they had anything to say about it. Angela somehow caught wind of what was going on and demanded that I put an end to things. Personally, I think she was more jealous than outraged."

I couldn't believe what I was hearing. Lori seemed like a snoop but she didn't strike me as smart enough to be manipulative. There was nothing about her story that she was ashamed of. Her words rolled off her tongue like sweat from a brow on a hot summer day, which led me to believe if I leaked this information then she would surely have something up her sleeve for me. I sat hushed as she went on.

"You can imagine my surprise when one morning I came into the office to find Bertha sitting in what I thought would be my seat. Apparently, I wasn't the only one that was willing to do whatever it took to get what I wanted. And even more apparent, the wives didn't have anything to say about me getting the position. As time passed, I sat back and watched everyone, specifically the bosses and their administrative sidekicks. Angela was stung from not getting Bertha's job and she never failed to hide her resentment. Bertha was kind enough to return the antipathy with harsh words and even harsher threats.

They built an animosity for me to play on. When things became unbearable between the two, I sprung into action. That infamous memo is my work of art. I planted clues at both of their desks, pointing the finger at each of them, implying that one of the two had penned the note. I knew sooner or later that one of them would run to the department heads with the evidence. All I had to do was sit back and wait. It was a fail-safe plan. Angela knew everything there was to know about the office and Bertha was eager enough to prove her worth. Roswell and Dunning wouldn't get rid of either of them, for both personal and professional reasons; but they would see them in a different light if I had anything to do with it. After the whole episode died down, the execs slowly reduced Angela's workload until she was left with nothing more than the responsibility of picking up their morning cups of coffee. I guess you can thank me for those sixteen blocks you trek every day. Bertha, on the other hand, didn't exactly enjoy such a heavy influx of work, and to this day blames Angela for her inbox overflow. All that's left is for them to duke it out on company time and BAM, I'm a shoe in for the job! Next on my list are those wives. They gave me a conference room table full of broken promises."

I was astounded by her conspiracy. Lori left no stone unturned. She was ruthless, vindictive, heartless, and precise. Even if she'd gotten caught, I don't think she'd be afraid. It was kind of sexy.

"What would happen if the memo ever got traced back to you?" I asked.

"It can't be traced back to me. I typed the letter on Bertha's computer and saved a copy onto Angela's. Then I deleted the file on both computers, leaving the documents swimming in recycle bin limbo. If either of them comes to me, all I'll have to do is retrieve what was deleted. If Roswell or Dunning decide to come at me wrong for any reason, I'll spill the beans to their wives about their two-on-one meetings with Bertha, or better yet, with each other. All my bases are covered."

After Lori's conspired story, I concluded that the real devil in the office was her. Unlike Bertha, she didn't need to screw her way to the top. She would have gotten there just fine on her own screwing everyone over. This dame's balls were just as big as her boobs. I had to be another pawn in her game because I couldn't for the life of me figure out what made her so comfortable sharing her evil stratagem. She knew I was becoming relatively close to Bertha yet she wasn't afraid of me knowing all the details of her plot. She had something up her sleeve and I didn't know what it was, nor was I trying to stick around to find out. This bitch is crazy. Security!

‡

Dear Hottywood,

Every day my coworker tells me about her relationship problems. Not only do I believe it is inappropriate conversation for the office, but I really just don't care! What can I do to make her stop?

Confidential

Dear Confidential,

First, I have to challenge your comment about the office being an inappropriate place to discuss relationship problems. People do it all the time [at work]: in the bathroom, in the cafeteria, at the water cooler, and in staff meetings. Work and relationship problems kind of go hand in hand. At any rate, you've already stated what the real issue is. You don't care about her problems. I won't give you the rundown of how your listening ear can be a saving grace to someone who may be in desperate need to talk or vent. Nor will I tell you that your way of thinking can be considered selfish and somewhat hypocritical when it comes time for you to lay down your burdens to anyone who's not standing on the other side of the mirror. I also won't bother to tell you that karma always comes back to bite you in the ass. I won't tell you these things because I'm pretty sure that you already know.

Realistically speaking, some people just can't help themselves. No matter how much of a disgustingly, uninterested face you can muster up, a person with that much self-absorption is usually more consumed with hearing words come out of their mouth than they are with focusing on the blood that's oozing out of your ears (not considering the preposterous notion that your ears are bleeding because of them). This act isn't uncommon and it doesn't just happen in the workplace. Outside of risking the possibility of breaking someone's heart by outright letting them know that you don't give a damn about what they're confiding in you, you have three other options:

- Offer a one-night stand word of advice. Tell her that "all fish are forgotten when they've either been flushed down the toilet or fried in a skillet." Don't offer any further explanation. That statement will have her baffled for the rest of the day.
- Protect yourself with common weaponry. The next time your coworker comes to you with her problems, arm yourself with a scorching hot cup of coffee. Toss it on her and start speaking in tongues. Dance frantically in place and spin

around in circles. Tell her, "Somebody in this room has been possessed!" and then run like the wind.
- Death by appetizer: Take her out to lunch. Once you've been seated, scotch-tape her to her chair and shoot her to death with a crossbow made from asparagus tips and onion rings. If she's still alive after that, do yourself a favor and dive head first into the nearest pitcher of water and drown yourself until the only voice you hear is God's.

If you're too soft or too scared to tell her that you'd rather not discuss her problems [in the office or any other place on the planet], then your last resort is to tell her you're super busy and request that she email you her stories. That way, you can read the first and last paragraph to sum up what she's whining about. Having her email you her problems is also a perfect setup for a paper trail leading back to her, which has all the promise of showing her employers that she's bringing her problems to the office, distracted by outside influences, and distracting her fellow coworkers from doing their job . . . all of which brings down the high rate percentage of work in the office.

Nothing much changed in the next month or so. Angela and Bertha continued to collide, Roswell and Dunning recapitulated their weekly closed door meetings with their wives, and Lori sat back and watched all the action unfold. It had gotten to a point where I came to work just to see whose skeletons would fall out of the closet first.

Every time Lori witnessed Bertha and I taking a noon day rest in the cafeteria, she ran her forefinger cross the bottom of her chin, implying a slice to my throat if I let the cat out of the bag. Bertha sensed my uneasiness. I wanted to tell her what I knew because she had grown to be a friend, but I didn't because I didn't want Lori to sneak up and murder me inside a bathroom stall.

"What's the matter with you?" Bertha put down her onion ring and looked straight into my eyes. "Why do you get all jittery when that dingbat walks by? Don't tell you me you like her. Or do you like her titties?"

I smiled nervously. If ever there were a time to have teleportation abilities, it was now. My eyes looked in every direction except Bertha's, each time shifting back to Lori, who always managed to stay in my line of view. The necktie around my neck tightened with every gulp of spit I swallowed. I had a better chance of surviving had I been hung from an apple tree. I answered Bertha as calmly as I could, vaguely realizing my words were beginning to ramble.

"Dingbats? I love dingbats. Not love as in love. Not that I have anything against love. I mean don't get me wrong, love is great. Wait, what was the question?"

Bertha's eyes called my bluff.

"I'm fine, B, seriously. I…I (think, Hottywood)… I have cramps." I don't know where I came up with that one liner but it certainly changed the tune of Bertha's question (although I'm not quite sure if the tune changed in my favor). Certainly hearing a man say he has cramps was nothing Bertha, or any woman for that matter, had ever heard before. Luckily there was at least one day in high school where I decided to sit through a whole session of biology class instead of dodging the truancy officer. I may have been lying at the moment, but I sure knew what the hell I was talking about.

Dear Hottywood,

I recently got into a pretty bad argument with my girlfriend. The argument resulted in her telling me that I'm acting like a real !@%# on her period. That got me to thinking. I notice that we get into the smallest arguments that escalate into the biggest deals, at least twice a month. My question to you is, "Do men have periods?"

Man Cramps

Dear Man Cramps,

Have you ever wondered why you've wanted to punch an alarm clock or a meter maid? Curse out your girlfriend, baby mama or some random stranger on the street for no apparent reason? Well I've got three words for you: Irritable Male Syndrome (IMS), aka, male PMS! So, Man Cramps, in answer to your question, "Yes, men do have periods."

 A man's period doesn't operate on the same cycle as a woman's because obviously we have no uterus. Our cycles are rather more sporadic, depending on the drop in levels of the hormone testosterone in our system. Like PMS for women, IMS comes with a wet, paper bag full of symptoms that include irritability, mood swings, hot flashes, depression, anger, feelings of anxiety, hypersensitivity, headaches, backaches, and even stomach cramps. Because IMS is caused by falls in levels of testosterone, there can also be a result of lack of sexual arousal and sexual dysfunction.

Actually, there have been a number of studies conducted on animals focusing on male PMS. One such study was tested on [male] sheep. In the study, scientists noted that the testosterone levels in the sheep were highest in the autumn months, during which time the male sheep experienced an increase in mating activity. In the winter months, hormone levels dropped dramatically and the sheep became nervous and anxious around females. The decrease in testosterone also caused the males to lash out at one another.

If you think that your acting like an asshole is a result of you going through your "male monthly," there is something you can do about it. Sometimes IMS symptoms can be alleviated with a topical [male progesterone] cream. Other suggestions that will help keep your shit under control is to make sure you have a sufficient amount of calcium and magnesium in your system. You can curtail your bitchiness by getting on a more health conscious diet. Lay off burgers, fries, and stadium hotdogs and try to stick with more healthy choices of food (10% saturated fat, 25% fat, 35% low glycemic carbohydrates (carbohydrates that are digested slowly and that do not cause insulin levels to spike) and 40% protein). This simple diet will keep your girlfriend from secretly telling all her friends that you're just a little girl trapped in a man's body. With this plan, approximately 30 to 40 minutes of exercise each day, 6 to 8 hours of sleep each night, and a lot of sexual attention from your girl when she isn't turned off by your feminine emotions, you can reduce the symptoms of IMS, stabilize your hormones, and get back to wearing the pants in your relationship. In my days of high school and college, two courses that I never missed and always aced were lunch and nutrition. Firstly, because food was the one language I could speak the best and secondly, I always seemed to have a thing for lunch ladies. You'd be surprised how far a smile and a compliment on a greasy apron can you get with a lunch lady.

Anyway, my dealings with cafeteria crews, coupled with my yearning to learn more about the kinds of foods I eat – thanks to the late Mrs. Zenobia Hamheister, nutrition professor at the College of Itchy Knuckles – gave me an opportunity to appreciate the value of a well-balanced diet, though that never shied me away from a good burger a few times a week. She had the most engaging nutrition classes, which could be because she used real food samples for her weekly lessons, but that's neither here nor there.

I remember Mrs. Hamheister constantly warning me to be careful of the kinds of food I eat because everything obviously isn't good for me, and also that certain foods can affect one's mood (enter Irritable Male Syndrome). I couldn't help but find truth in that statement because burgers, fries and chicken wings always made me happy, while I found myself saddest when I had none of the three. This explained a lot about my mood swings and required a little more research on my part, so I did a little digging into the subject and stumbled upon a then little medical website where I was able to delve deeper into the logistics of IMS, its causes, effects and treatments. The knowledge that I picked up never left me, and because of that I've been able to tuck my man period in my back pocket whenever I wanted to ingest a trough of chocolate and cry at the drop of a dime. Between you and me, though, I still cry at the drop of a dime. Times are hard these. I'm sure I'm not the only man that cries when his pockets are empty and that has nothing to do with a period – male or female's.

Lori must have felt Bertha's suspicion. I could feel her cold glare heating up. I tried to muffle my nervous breakdown by stuffing a handful of breadcrumbs into my mouth but that didn't do anything but make me thirsty. I couldn't take it anymore. My nerves could have been a spokesperson for a Jenny Craig commercial as thin as they got. I twitched. My knees clanked under the table and a gross sweat stain unattractively pervaded the armpits of my polo. Bertha wasn't buying the distraction.

"What the hell is wrong with you?"

If I were a witness on a confession stand my testimony would have surely sent someone to jail.

"I have something to tell you." She leaned in closer, eager to learn what had me so unraveled. Just as I was about to cave under the pressure, guess who decided to join us.

"Lori! Look, Bertha. It's Lori! Lori, what are you doing here?"

Lori's smile was dramatically bright. Too bright. Mr. Potato Head bright. As she placed her lunch tray on the table, she reached for the steak knife that rested beside her grilled sirloin and waved it freely.

For some reason she reminded me of a female Norman Bates.

"You two looked like you were having such a good time. I couldn't resist the temptation of coming over to get in on the fun. I hope that's not a problem. Hottywood." She asked, "is that a problem?"

"No, no. Not a problem at all. In fact, take my seat. I just remembered there's something I have to do."

"What's that?" Lori hung on the edge of my words. She found pleasure in my discomfort.

"Quit!"

And with that final response, I gathered my things and marched my ass over to Human Resources to turn in my resignation. All the money in the world wasn't enough to keep me trapped in someone's pocket. My taste of victory came with an unscathed escape. I never went back to the office after that day. I never heard from Bertha or Lori again, and I don't know what ever came of their running soap opera. To tell you the truth, I didn't want to know. I had too many secrets to keep from being in the wrong places with the wrong people off the clock. I couldn't double that guilt from 9 to 5. I wasn't ready for that. I wasn't strong enough or smart enough, not to mention getting paid enough.

Until that particular episode, Mama's reminder of the necessity to know and understand the five senses of survival in the office didn't resonate with me. I never suspected that I would deal with that level of connivance in a professional setting. If I didn't learn anything else in the short span of time working with the staff of Lazy Heifer Couch Potato Productions, I learned never to underestimate power hungry people.

Obviously, it wasn't long after that I landed a new job. After experiencing a few more personalities in a few more agencies across the city, I quickly realized that the workplace is filled with just as many crazy people as are in the streets. Lori isn't the only employee in the world with psychotic tendencies. In fact, most organizations are filled with workers that claw their way to the top. The trick before starting any new gig is to remember to expect the unexpected. You may be greeted with a plastic smile, a cup of yesterday's coffee and a staff meeting that would be more efficient if conducted by email; but no amount of standard office procedure will ever prepare you for the hot water that's cooked up at the water cooler.

‡

After about four and a half hours of listening to Hottywood's anecdotes, Graños de Café looked like a ghost town. Hector was operating on auto pilot. The sumo wrestler that entertained the outside neighbors earlier finally found himself rested inside the café over a chilled glass of Jack Daniels Whiskey Tea and Lemon minus the tea and the lemon. Hottywood's cup never emptied as he put the final topping on the stories he served up. My eyes wouldn't have been far from closed if it weren't for the giggles of his tales. In fact, my mind would have been closed if it weren't for those tales.

I wondered to myself why he wasn't a complete basket case. He'd been through some adventures whether he was the cause, the cure or just a piece of the puzzle. Then it dawned on me that he was who he was because he accepted that he wasn't the only crazy person on the planet. He never separated himself from the world (except for his immediate stage exit from Lazy Heifer Couch Potato Productions) and he reminded people that being different is normal, as are bad luck and awful experiences. That's what draws people to him. That's what makes his advice so warranted. That's why no matter how far I run, I always find my way back to him. He really is just like everyone else. He's been through what others have gone through, and he helps everyone to realize that there's nothing wrong with being different. Even me. Especially me. I think he always knew that, which is why he chose me to be his emotional channel. I needed to know it as much as he knew it.

We as a people experience things both good and bad. Sometimes we laugh. Sometimes we cry. Sometimes we throw rocks, punches and bean pies. But we learn from our experiences, and as long as they don't involve getting run over by an Amtrak train, we live to tell the story of our survival.

As it turned out, having a face to face with Hottywood was exactly what I needed to take a hard look at myself. Seeing a vision through someone else's eyes made me see that sometimes you have to close your eyes in order to see what's really in front of you. Some men call it hope. Some call it blind faith. I call it sleep walking. But mostly I call it bracing yourself for getting hit with cold hard reality. Whatever it's called, it's life. You don't know what you can handle until you're forced to face the facts.

So as I sit back and think about the last police car and jail cell that Hottywood inadvertently dragged me into, I realize that I lived. I survived some bad times and I learned to laugh about it another day. I can appreciate the humor in unfunny things, though I pray that shit never happens to me again. I can accept perfectly my imperfections and live comfortably knowing that I'm not alone. In fact a perfect man is imperfect in his belief that he holds no flaws. For no one can evolve if there is nothing more to gain. Relationships can't grow. Jobs can't become careers. There's nothing to look forward to; nothing left to hit but a wall.

I think I can safely speak for both myself and Hottywood when I encourage people not to worry so much about the bad choices they make because in the end all of our steps are ordered. And even though there are those that make bad choices by nature, it isn't for not. The lessons that we learn from whatever choices we make come at a price more valuable for what we get out of them rather than the price we pay. Those lessons are necessary for the evolution of maturity; for self-growth; for self-evaluation; for I told you so's. They are the process of finding out what one is made of; an appreciation for an outcome of something believed to be incapable of survival. I wouldn't have known that if it wasn't for Hottywood. If his unorthodox storytelling and advice proves nothing to no one else, it proves to me that Hottywood Helps.

Hottywood Extras

SELF-EVALUATION QUIZ

It's never easy to accept that you have flaws, despite the flaws anyone may point out. Luckily for you, Hottywood Helps! This little quiz will help you to realize that your ass is not as perfect as you think. Be warned that the truth hurts. But in the end, truth never hurt so good.

1. **Do you feel your best when . . .**
   A. You find yourself hooked up to an IV full of brandy infused-coffee?
   B. You're too drunk to know where the hell you are?
   C. Your nipples are hardest?
   D. You've awakened in a strange bed after a drunken romp with a horny, one-eyed stud muffin from a Kansas City trailer park?
   E. When someone almost, sort of kind of boosts your ego a little?
   F. Never. You're the complete opposite of "life of the party."

2. **When talking to people, do you . . .**
   A. Spit excessively?
   B. Blink excessively?
   C. Stare at boobs?
   D. Avoid direct eye and breath contact?

E. Let your underarms do all the talking?

F. None of the above. You never speak to anyone because people say it sounds as if you have a mouth full of caramel.

3. When you go to a party or social gathering, do you . . .

A. Sneak in the back door naked?

B. Make a loud and obnoxious entrance so everyone will have a legitimate reason to avoid you all night?

C. Announce the pee stain on your pants is because you couldn't find the bathroom?

D. French kiss all of the other guests after eating a personal-sized, onion pizza?

E. Belch out of the wrong end when you laugh uncontrollably?

F. None of the above. You never get invited to parties.

4. When you go to a public restaurant, do you . .

A. Chew with your mouth open because it's more convenient to ingest more food?

B. Belch without saying "excuse me" (although there's nothing wrong with that unless you're a midget. Then it's just wrong.)?

C. Order the most expensive meal on the menu knowing that you're flat broke?
D. Accidentally forget to wear pants on purpose?
E. Steal the utensils when the meal is over?
F. None of the above. You've been banned from public eating establishments for reasons known only to you, God and your imaginary friend?

5. When you are bored, do you . . .
A. Make prank phone calls to old people and Chinese sheep herders?
B. Clean the lint out of your belly button?
C. Speak backwards while groping your private parts or the private parts of the person to whom you are speaking?
D. Try to sing at a frequency only dogs can hear, like Mariah Carey and Minnie Riperton?
E. Make plans with more than one person knowing damn well you don't have enough gas in your car to make it pass the hooker on the corner at the top of the hill, let alone be in two places at one time?
F. None of the above. With the all the voices in your head, you never get bored.

If you were able to answer any of these questions, then you are not fit to live among normal people.

Don't be ashamed. There's someone out there just as ridiculous as you are. Maybe worse. Maybe not.

EMPLOYMENT QUIZ

There comes a moment in everyone's life where they must decide if their current place of employment is where they want to build their career or use it as a stepping stone towards their dream job. This is never an easy decision to make. Luckily for you, Hottywood Helps! This little quiz will help you to realize how much intolerance you are able to endure from your current job and coworkers before finally flipping your desk upside down, setting it ablaze and roasting marshmallows by the flames. Be warned that the truth hurts, but in the end truth never hurt so good.

1. How would you go about handling your first day at the office?
   A. Smile brightly and answer "yes" to every question asked of you.
   B. Roll your eyes at everyone whose butt is bigger than yours.
   C. Use your camera phone to snap pictures of everyone you think will be on your shit list by the end of the week.
   D. Always appear as if you know what you're talking about, even at the risk of sounding like an obnoxious know-it-all.

E. Shimmy your boobs in your colleagues' face in hopes of making a lasting first impression [man boobs included].
   F. All of the above.

2. **One of your colleagues makes an advance towards you. Do you . . .**
   A. Punch them in the esophagus?
   B. Contact your manager and ask if it's okay to have conjugal visits during one of your 15 minute breaks?
   C. Contact Boo Boo and Half Pint and tell them you'll offer them $20 each to beat up your colleague in the parking lot after hours?
   D. Contact your husband/wife and tell him/her you'll be home late for dinner?
   E. Buy new underwear and conveniently forget to wear a belt?
   F. All of the above.

3. **One of your colleagues insists on telling you intimate details of their personal life. Do you...**
   A. Scotch-tape their lips to the shredder machine?
   B. Use sticky pad glue to paste your ears shut?
   C. Fax yourself to another part of the office?
   D. Put white-out in their coffee creamer?

E. Tell them to send you the details of their story via email so you can run a paper trail. Blind carbon-copy their manager on the emails and suggest an impromptu employment performance review?

F. All of the above.

4. **You have been working tirelessly on a project for three weeks. During your office staff meeting, a colleague takes the credit for all of your work. Do you . . .**
   A. Fire a round of paperclips at the corporate thief using nothing but a rubber band and a box of rusted paperclips dipped in stale powdered donut crumbs?
   B. Karate-chop the colleague in the neck, write the word 'liar' on his/her forehead one hundred times with a permanent magic marker and then tell him/her the devil made you do it?
   C. Stick gum in the colleague's hair?
   D. Super glue all of the files together that rests in the colleague's inbox?
   E. Be a punk and quit?
   F. All of the above.

5. **You don't feel like going into the office. Do you . . .**

A. Call out sick? Be truthful when telling the appropriate person(s) that you are sick and tired of being sick and tired.
B. Call out sick? Lie through your teeth and hope whomever you've shared your bogus excuse with is dumb enough to believe whatever story you've concocted.
C. Call the office and disguise your voice? Tell them you've set stink bombs throughout the building that are scheduled to go off at random times of the day. Warn them that the stink bombs are laced with hot morning breath and will cause all computer keyboards to melt.
D. Ram your car into the side of your office building and watch it collapse from the inside?
E. Quit?

If you were able to answer any of these questions, congratulations! You are ready to take on the work force. And just think. You'll have about 30 or 40 years to fuck up before old age brings you to the doorstep of retirement.